"Jordan, you didn't
used to be so severe."

"Do you mean ten years ago?" Jordan's
voice had risen a little in spite of her
effort to control her reaction. "I was a
child then. Or had you forgotten?"

"I hadn't forgotten," Rhys said wearily.
"This may be difficult for you to
believe, but when I saw you again,
I realized I didn't hate you
anymore...."

"You...hated...me?" Jordan almost
choked on the words.

"Did you expect my gratitude for
walking out on me like that?"

"And did you expect me to stay around
and *share* you with your wife?"

Ten years of nurturing her hatred
could not be dispelled in one night...
even though every nerve in her body
was still sensitive to the subtle
sexuality he exuded.

Books by Anne Mather

STORMSPELL
WILD CONCERTO

HARLEQUIN PRESENTS

HARLEQUIN ROMANCES

These books may be available at your local bookseller.

For a list of all titles currently available,
send your name and address to:

Harlequin Reader Service
P.O. Box 52040, Phoenix, AZ 85072-2040
Canadian address: P.O. Box 2800, Postal Station A,
5170 Yonge St., Willowdale, Ont. M2N 5T5

ANNE MATHER

moondrift

Harlequin Books

TORONTO • NEW YORK • LONDON
AMSTERDAM • PARIS • SYDNEY • HAMBURG
STOCKHOLM • ATHENS • TOKYO • MILAN

Harlequin Presents first edition August 1984
ISBN 0-373-10715-3

Original hardcover edition published in 1984
by Mills & Boon Limited

Printed in U.S.A.

CHAPTER ONE

THE island lay almost immediately below the plane now, one of a group of smaller islands that depended on the larger islands for most of their supplies. It grew coconut palms and banana plants and pineapples, and a small amount of sugar cane, but mostly it relied on tourism for its survival, which at times had not been easy. Shaped like an avocado, it lay drowsing beneath the heat of a Caribbean afternoon, and Rhys felt his nerves tightening as the Cessna banked to make its landing.

He had not wanted to come back. Indeed, there were times when he had sworn he would never come back. But it was ten years now, ten years and he had finally got the island out of his blood. He had had to come back to complete the catharsis.

'Is that Eleutha, Daddy?'

The girl beside him leaned towards the window excitedly, gazing down at the oblong curve of sand that fringed the west coast of the island. The hotel was situated along that strip of beach, Rhys remembered unwillingly, its low-walled terrace overlooking the lagoon confined by the reef.

'Yes, that's Eleutha,' he answered now, giving her a brief smile. 'We'll be landing in a couple of minutes. You'd better get your things together.'

'I've only got my bag and my jacket,' she exclaimed, looking down at her bare legs with some satisfaction. 'Look, I'm getting brown already. I expect to have a really super tan when we get back to London.'

Rhys regarded her with affection. 'You're not

5

wanting to go back already, are you?' he enquired, and she shook her head.

'No, of course not. You said we could stay for a month, didn't you?' Her dark gold eyes, so like his own, sparkled excitedly. 'I can't wait to see our house. Does it really have its own stretch of beach?'

'It does.' Rhys's eyes turned irresistibly towards the window again. 'I just hope you don't get bored. Eleutha isn't London, and there are no discothèques or department stores here.'

'That's not fair!' A sulky look invaded her eyes at his faint criticism. 'I didn't get bored when we went to Mauritius, did I? And you were working there. You're not going to work here, are you? You promised!'

Rhys sighed. 'I said, if I remember correctly, that I didn't think I'd feel like working here,' he corrected her drily. 'Besides, you won't want my company all the time. I'm too old.'

'You're not old,' she contradicted him fiercely. 'You're only thirty-six!'

'Exactly twenty years older than you, madame,' he retorted shortly, squashing the remembrance that Jordan had only been a year older than Lucy when he first came to the island. 'Anyway,' he pushed these thoughts aside, 'if you do get bored, we can always go back to Nassau.'

'I shan't.' She gazed through the window in delight. 'I don't know how you could bear to stay away all these years. Look at the water! Isn't it absolutely fantastic!'

'Fantastic,' agreed Rhys, though his lips twisted as the Cessna's wheels made contact with the runway. He shouldn't have come, an inner voice was warning him. He should have sold the house ten years ago, instead of allowing it to stand like a silent monument to his own folly.

The pilot turned as the plane taxied to a halt near the whitewashed building that acted as both service and administration. 'Glad to be back, Mr Williams?' he enquired, giving the girl beside his employer a teasing wink. 'Nothing's changed, as you can see. Here comes Jacob, eager to shake you by the hand.'

Rhys grinned, forcing himself to relax, and levered his long lean body out of his seat. 'We're all ten years older,' he remarked, thrusting open the Cessna's door and letting down the flight of steps. 'Come on, Lucy, let's go and find the jeep.'

Lucy needed no second bidding, her eyes wide with excitement. Bidding the pilot a swift farewell, she followed her father down the steps, looking about her eagerly as he exchanged greetings with the coloured man who had come to meet them.

The airstrip was situated near to a sandy beach, not the beach they had seen from the plane, but the narrower strip of sand that formed the northern boundary. Even so, the sight of the fine white powdered grains bordered by the creaming surf was quite beautiful, and she tugged Rhys's arm impatiently when he seemed disposed to linger.

'You remember Lucy, don't you?' Rhys remarked with a wry smile, and the old man who had had charge of the small airport for the past fifteen years gave him a doubtful look.

'*This* is Lucy?'

'It is.' Rhys glanced around as if familiarising himself anew with his surroundings. But the truth was, he didn't want to get into a discussion about his daughter, and cutting Jacob off, he said: 'Is the jeep here?'

The old man looked doubtful, but as he did so, another, younger man, came sauntering across the tarmac towards them. 'Well, here comes Tomas now,' he observed, evidently relieved. 'Late, as usual, but generally reliable.'

'Good afternoon, Mr Williams, sir,' the younger man exclaimed now, his dark eyes taking in Rhys's jean-clad figure and Lucy's Bermudas with one sweeping glance. 'It's good to have you back. Rosa's talked of nothing else for days.'

'Really?' Rhys introduced his daughter to the man, who with his wife, had stayed on as caretakers at the house. Like Jacob, Tomas had lived all his life on the island, and Rhys realised it had been a futile hope that their arrival here should have remained unannounced. Rosalie was too keen on gossiping for that and, he reflected, somewhat philosophically, it was probably better that way. There was less chance of running into Jordan if she knew he was here. He had little doubt that she would want to stay out of his way, too.

The pilot had hauled their cases out of the Cessna, and now Rhys hefted Lucy's overnight bag and his own guitar case while Tomas took charge of the suitcases. Then, together, they crossed the uneven surface of the runway to where an ancient ex-army jeep stood waiting in the shadow of a clump of palms.

'It still runs, eh?' remarked Rhys, swinging the bags into the back and hoisting Lucy up into the front seat.

'As ever,' agreed Tomas, joining the cases in the back, and grimacing, Rhys slid behind the wheel.

The road from the airport ran parallel with the coast for some way, then took a winding track among fields tall with sugar cane. Huge sticks of it had fallen into the road in places, causing the jeep to buck a little as it bounced over the obstacle, and there was the sweet smell of rain in the air, indicating a morning shower.

'You have a good journey, Mr Williams?' asked Tomas, clinging tenaciously to the back of their seats, and Rhys nodded.

'We only flew from Nassau this afternoon,' he explained. 'We came down from Miami on Thursday.'

'Ah,' Tomas nodded. 'I thought Miss Lucy looked like she'd been doin' some sunbathing. Plenty of time for that here,' he added, as the girl cast him a careless look. 'Not much else to do, really, less'n you like to swim or sail.'

'I do,' declared Lucy impatiently, giving her father an appealing look. 'Is it much further, Daddy? I can't wait to get there!'

The roads around the island were delightfully quiet after Nassau. Apart from the occasional bicycle, and one or two cattle-drawn vehicles, they didn't see another car, and Rhys regretted Lucy's impatience when he was feeling an unfamiliar sense of identity with his surroundings.

'It's not much more than a mile now,' he said, taking his eyes from the road for a moment. 'You can see the ocean through the trees if you look. Our house is only a few yards from the beach.'

Lucy strained her eyes to see, and Rhys allowed the little jeep to coast the last few yards to their turning. It was all so familiar, he could hardly believe it was more than ten years since he had driven here. *So long as he remembered it was*, he reminded himself harshly.

A narrow drive, overhung with the scarlet beauty of hibiscus, gave access to a gravelled forecourt. Lucy was already exclaiming her enthusiasm before she saw the cream-washed walls of the house, and impulsively she hugged him as he brought the jeep to a standstill.

'It's beautiful!' she cried, jumping excitedly out of the vehicle. 'Oh, I didn't expect anything like this! You said it would most likely be overgrown with weeds and falling to bits!'

Rhys cast Tomas a rueful look. 'I didn't exactly say that, Lucy,' he protested, though he admitted he was pleasantly surprised at the condition of the place. Tomas and Rosalie had evidently gone to some trouble to keep the house and grounds in good order, and Lucy's careless candour grated a little. 'I just said everything grew like mad, and that termites ran riot in the islands. But apparently,' he looked at the other man again, 'you've done a good job.'

'Oh, Missy Jordan made sure everythin' stayed the way it should,' Tomas responded airily, sliding off the tailboard, evidently unaware of the bombshell he had delivered. 'And here comes Rosa now. See, they're here—all safe and sound!'

In the genuine pleasure of the housekeeper's greeting, Rhys was able to keep other thoughts at bay, at least temporarily, and Rosalie's ample arms engulfed him in an enveloping embrace. 'I couldn't believe it when Tomas told me you were comin' back here, Mr Williams,' she exclaimed, her voice echoing the sentiment that was evident in her moist brown eyes. 'It's good to have you back. Ain't had no one to cook for in ages.'

'You got me,' put in Tomas goodhumouredly, but Rosalie only sniffed, her round face wobbling with emotion.

'You're so thin,' she exclaimed, her fingers clutching the lapels of Rhys's shirt. 'Got to do somethin' about that, and soon!'

Rhys managed a faint smile, and extracting himself from her clinging fingers, he drew a reluctant Lucy forward. 'What do you think of my daughter?' he demanded, his hand resting proudly on the girl's shoulder. 'Quite a transformation from the infant you remember, hmm?'

'This is Lucy?' Rosalie cast her eyes heavenward for a moment. 'My, my, hasn't she grown? And so pretty?' She subjected the girl to another of her suffocating squeezes. 'You and me's goin' to be good friends, Lucy. Just like me and Missy Jordan, when she was younger.'

Rhys noticed that Lucy quickly extricated herself from the woman's hold, and the look she cast in his direction was unmistakable. She didn't like Tomas and Rosalie's familiarity, and although he sympathised with the strangeness she must be feeling, he wished she had been a little more friendly.

'Can we go inside, Daddy?' she pleaded. 'I can't wait to see my room. And I want to have a swim before I change for dinner.'

'I guess so.' Rhys bent to pick up the guitar case he had put down to return Rosalie's welcome, and gestured towards the house. 'You lead the way. Just follow the path round to the verandah. It's not difficult to find.'

Lucy needed no second bidding, and Rosalie raised her hands in understanding when Rhys cast her an apologetic glance. 'Go ahead, Mr Williams,' she declared, nodding in approbation. 'It's good to know you haven't forgotten the old place.'

Forgotten? Rhys wondered if he would ever forget, as he followed his daughter along the paved path that circled the colour-washed wall of the house. There were too many things to remind him, not least Lucy herself, but she had no idea of the depths of feeling behind this visit. To her it was just a house her father had bought and which she had visited once when she was a very small child. She didn't understand her father's aversion for the place, or the reasons why they had never come back here. She simply saw it as a second home, that her father had chosen not to use.

When he reached the front of the building, Lucy was already on the slatted boards of the verandah, testing the cushioned seat of a bamboo lounger. 'Isn't it wonderful, Daddy?' she exclaimed, gesturing at the view, and Rhys turned to survey the sweep of sun-kissed beach and green-gold water that spread out before them.

'Wonderful!' he echoed briefly, climbing the steps with grim determination, and Lucy looked at him consideringly as he paused before speaking to her.

'I thought you wanted to see your room,' he said at last, advancing to where folding shutters gave access to the room beyond. He propped the shaft of his guitar case against his shoulder and drew a steadying breath. 'This is the living room, and that's the dining room through the arch.'

'I thought it must be.' Lucy left her perch to come and join him, linking her arm with his. 'Is it exactly as you remembered?'

'More or less.' Rhys was offhand, but he couldn't help it. 'Let's go inside, shall we?'

Lucy shrugged. 'What's the matter?' She was perceptive. 'Why are you looking like that? Did I do something wrong?'

'You?' Rhys looked at her strangely, then his face cleared and he released her arm to hug her close against his side. 'No, you didn't do anything wrong,' he assured her gently. And then, hearing Tomas and Rosalie's voices as they came along the path, he drew her into the artificially-darkened room.

The house was comfortably simple in design. There were six rooms on the ground floor and six rooms on the upper one. As well as the living and dining rooms, there was a kind of studio, which Rhys had used as a music room in the past, as well as the kitchen, and bathroom, and Tomas and Rosalie's bedroom. A cool tiled hallway ran from front to back of the house, with a shallow, curving stairway giving access to the upper floor.

Rhys spent little time showing Lucy around downstairs. 'You'll soon find your way about,' he assured her, leading the way upstairs, and Lucy scampered up after him, matching two of her steps to his agile stride.

There were three bedrooms and three bathrooms on the first floor. Two of the bedrooms overlooked the curve of beach, and the third embraced the sweep of the drive and the glowing hibiscus blossom.

'Which would you like?' asked Rhys, allowing Lucy to make her choice. To his relief she chose the larger of the two ocean-facing rooms, thus removing any necessity for him to refuse that particular apartment. Even entering the translucent beauty of the bedroom evoked the most painful memories he had experienced so far, and he was glad when Lucy pushed open the louvred doors and he could step out on to the balcony.

'Isn't it unbelievable?' she exclaimed, leaning on the wrought iron rail. 'Oh, how could you neglect the place for so long?'

'I haven't had the time,' Rhys responded, keeping his tone purposely light. 'Besides, there are places I like more. Islands in the Pacific, for example.'

Lucy grimaced. 'Oh, well, I suppose you have been busy,' she conceded. Then she turned and rested her elbows over the rail. 'But are you sure you don't mind me having this room? It is the biggest room, isn't it?'

'The one at the back is just as big,' replied Rhys quickly. 'Besides, I don't need a big room.' He grinned. 'I don't have half a dozen suitcases of clothes to accommodate.'

'Oh, you!'

Lucy dug him playfully in the ribs, then sighed half impatiently when she heard Tomas labouring into the bedrooms behind them. 'I'll leave these in here, shall I, Mr Williams?' he called, attracting his employer's attention, and Rhys strolled back into the room to give him his instructions.

'Those two are mine,' Rhys said swiftly. 'Put them in next door, would you, Tomas? I'll deal with them later.'

'But isn't this your room, Mr Williams?' Tomas protested in some surprise. 'Seems like I remember, last time you were here——'

'Not this time,' asserted Rhys crisply, passing him to reach the landing and walking into the other ocean-facing bedroom. 'This will do me fine, Tomas. Put Miss Lucy's cases in next door.'

'As you say, Mr Williams.'

Tomas's dark brows ascended with some disapproval, but he didn't argue. After depositing Rhys's luggage on the rack provided, he disappeared downstairs again for the rest of their belongings, and Rhys pushed his hands into the pockets of his jeans in a gesture of repudiation.

'Isn't this cosy?'

Lucy's sudden appearance from the balcony they both shared interrupted his mood, and forcing a corresponding smile to his lips, he inclined his head. 'Very,' he conceded, looking round the comfortable apartment. 'And if you can entertain yourself for the next few minutes, I'll go and have a word with Rosa and find out what the form is.'

'Can't I come with you?'

Lucy's face mirrored her disappointment, but Rhys had to speak to Rosa alone. 'You unpack,' he advised, accompanying the rebuff with a casual caress to her cheek. 'Find your swimsuit. There'll be plenty of time to test the water before dinner.'

Lucy looked mutinous, but she knew better than to argue with him in this mood. There was a certain compression about his mouth that warned of his uncertain temper, and his eyes, which were usually so warm and affectionate, now gleamed like molten amber.

'All right,' she said, going towards the bedroom door. 'But you will swim with me later, won't you?'

'I've said so, haven't I?' he responded, with that clipped edge to his voice, and Lucy dipped her head in acquiescence before making good her escape.

Left to himself, Rhys paused only long enough to cast one unwilling glance at the view beyond the windows before striding after his daughter. But whereas she had returned to the other bedroom, he quickly descended the stairs, walking surely along the tiled hallway to the airy pine-scented kitchen at the back of the house.

Rosalie was at the table, setting cups and saucers on to a polished wood tray, adding a cork stand and a rose-patterned teapot. She looked up when Rhys entered the room, but her eyes revealed no surprise. 'You want tea or something stronger?' she asked perceptively. 'I guessed you'd be coming to see Rosa before too long.'

'Something stronger,' said Rhys, gesturing towards the refrigerator. 'Have you got a beer or some lager? I seem to remember you kept quite a store in the old days.'

Rosa chuckled. 'Got some in, 'specially for you comin',' she declared, padding over to the fridge and fetching him an iced can. 'Sit down. Make yourself at home. We got a lot of years to make up.'

Rhys hesitated a moment and then he wedged his hip on a corner of the scrubbed table. Pulling the ring on the can, he watched the beer ooze out in a cluster of fizzy bubbles before saying quietly: 'What did Tomas mean about Jordan Lucas?'

'Missy Jordan?' Rosalie tried to sound offhand and failed. 'What did he tell you 'bout her?'

Rhys sighed, hazarding a guess that Rosalie had heard exactly what her husband said. But, deciding to play it their way, he explained patiently: 'About the house. About Miss Jordan making sure things stayed the way they should be. Are you telling me Jordan Lucas has visited here while I've been away?'

Involuntarily his voice had quickened, hardened, and Rosalie responded to it, spreading her hands wide as she endeavoured to justify the situation. 'She was just tryin' to be neighbourly,' she exclaimed. 'After all, this used to be her daddy's home when he was a little boy.'

'I know that.' Rhys's voice brooked no compromise. 'I bought it from Robert Lucas, remember? But it's mine now. It's not the Lucas house any more. And I don't know by what right you thought *she* had leave to come here in my absence!'

Rosalie wrung her hands now, her dark eyes rolling expressively. 'You have been away ten years, Mr Williams——'

'Is that supposed to be an excuse?'

'Yes. No. I don't know.' The housekeeper was getting more and more agitated. 'I didn't know I was doin' wrong. You and she were always so close, up until—up until——'

'Up until about three weeks before I left,' Rhys finished for her grimly. 'My God, I only kept the house open because of you!'

'Yes, sir.'

'And this is what happens!' He took a savage drink from the can. 'If I'd known Jordan Lucas was likely to come anywhere near this place, I'd have closed the house up, boarded the windows, locked the gates, and to hell with the sense of it!'

'Yes, sir.' Rosalie's bright good humour had been quenched. 'I understand.'

'Do you? Do you?' Rhys got up from the table and strode aggressively round the kitchen. 'I wonder.'

Rosalie shook her head. 'I didn't think you'd mind. And after her daddy died, and all——'

'Robert Lucas is dead?' Rhys swung round to face her.

'More'n six years ago,' nodded Rosalie quickly. 'He wasn't a well man, you know, and what with the accident and——'

'What accident?' Rhys's eyes narrowed. 'Jordan didn't have an accident, did she?'

'No, no.' Rosalie licked her thick lips. 'It was Mr Lucas. He almost drowned. Never did get over it.'

'What happened?' Rhys came back to the table and then, seeing the way Rosalie flinched away from him, he sighed. 'Please—I want to know what happened. Was it a sailing accident?'

'It was.' Rosalie folded her plump hands together. 'That boat of his capsized. He was in the water for hours. When they got him out he was pretty sick.'

Rhys absorbed this with brooding concentration. 'And—he died, afterwards.'

'Not then, no.' Rosalie made a negative gesture. 'The accident happened soon after you went away.'

'I see.' Rhys finished his beer and crushed the can in his fist. 'So has the hotel been sold?'

'No. Missy Jordan took over. She'd been helping her father for years, and it was natural that she should want to carry on.'

Rhys nodded. 'And—when did she start coming here?'

Rosalie hesitated. 'Missy Jordan's always come here. She loves this house. When you went away, she said to me, "Rosa," she said, "I want you to care for the house, just as if Mr Williams still lived here." And I have.'

Rhys expelled his breath heavily. 'Are you sure she didn't say, just as if Mr Lucas still lived here?' he inquired harshly. 'Oh, what the hell! It's done now.' He paused. 'And I am grateful to you and Tomas for looking after things so well.'

'Are you?' Rosalie sniffed. 'Seems like you don't care about us at all, only the house.'

Rhys shook his head. 'I'm sorry.' He ran restless fingers through the thick straight hair that sprung darkly from his scalp. 'But you have to understand my feelings, too. I don't like the idea of Jordan Lucas coming here. I don't want her on my property. I admit—once she was welcome here, but now she's not. And you can tell her that the next time you see her.'

'Yes, sir.'

Rosalie's response was polite, but unfriendly, and Rhys cursed Jordan anew for creating this unwanted hostility between himself and the housekeeper. It was natural that Rosalie should side with Jordan. She had worked for Jordan's grandfather before coming to work for him, and years ago he had been grateful to Jordan for providing him with such excellent staff. But that was all over now. The past was something he wanted to erase. And because of Jordan, he was being forced to face it far sooner than he had intended.

CHAPTER TWO

'HE'S back!'

Jordan was in the linen room counting pillowcases when Karen came to find her, and although she had been expecting it, her sister's words still brought out a wave of goosebumps over her skin.

'Who?' she asked, as if there could be any doubt, and Karen gazed at her disbelievingly.

'You know who!' she accused after a moment, propping herself against the door frame. 'The great man, of course. He arrived yesterday afternoon. With his daughter.'

Jordan felt the muscles of her stomach tense, and to disguise her emotions from Karen, she moved out of the shaft of sunlight cast through the door. Thank goodness she had an occupation, she thought sickly, as her heart palpitated wildly. It was worse, much worse, than she had imagined, and the fact that he had brought the child with him showed how insensitive he was.

'Well? Don't you have anything to say?' Karen was growing impatient, and she regarded her elder sister suspiciously. 'Did you know already?' she demanded suddenly. 'Did you know it was yesterday he was due? Or did your spies at the house let you know that your pop singer was here?'

'He's not my pop singer!' Jordan's voice was muffled, but audible. 'Karen, if you've nothing else to do, you can drive down to the town for those avocados. I shan't have time this morning, and Josef needs them for tonight.'

'Forget about the avocados!' Karen snorted. 'Jordan, I just told you that Rhys Williams is back on the island! Doesn't that mean anything to you?'

'What should it mean?' Making sure her face was still in shadow, Jordan turned to face her sister. 'My relationship with Rhys Williams ended over ten years ago. I—I was a child, that's all. It was a childish infatuation. It means nothing to me now.'

'So why do you spend every spare minute at his house?' demanded Karen scathingly. 'Since he went away, you've been there at least once every week. Come on, Jordan. I may have been a kid when it happened, but I'm not a kid now!'

Jordan pressed the clipboard holding the house-keeping lists close to her chest. 'You forget,' she said, hearing the tremor in her voice and despising herself for it, 'that house was Daddy's home, too. Is it so unnatural that I should want to make sure it didn't fall into disrepair?'

Karen shook her head. 'And that's your final word?'

'What do you mean?'

'I mean, I don't believe you,' retorted Karen succinctly, swinging about and making for the stairs. 'I'll get your avocados. I shan't be long.'

After she had gone, Jordan spent several minutes composing herself before emerging from the linen room. There was always the chance that someone else might take it into their heads to inform her of Rhys's return, and she wanted to be sure she could face their commiserations before returning to her office.

Just to make doubly sure, she made a detour to her own apartments, and closing the louvred door behind her, she paused a moment to take a deep breath. Rhys was back. Well, she had been expecting it. And it was nothing so terrible if she could keep things in perspective.

Walking across to her dressing table, she lifted a comb and lightly flicked back the errant strands that had escaped from the chignon at her nape. Her hair, which was toffee-coloured and streaked with blonde, grew back from a centre parting. Her brow was wide and tanned, and her eyes were grey and shielded by long brown lashes. She knew she was not beautiful in the accepted sense of the word, but when her features were animated they did have a certain attraction which she was not unaware of. Right now, however, her face was withdrawn and sombre, and she surveyed herself without pleasure and assessed the changes Rhys must see.

When he went away, she had been seventeen—now she was twenty-seven; a spinster, or so Karen was often telling her. As a teenager, she had worn her hair loose and free; now it was always coiled in a chignon or a knot, anything to keep it out of her eyes. And finally, when she was younger, her long-limbed frame had been rounded and feminine; these days, she seldom had an ounce of flesh on her bones, and she touched the hollows in her neck with fingers that shook quite revealingly.

Damn, she thought fiercely, turning away, why couldn't she just dismiss him from her mind? He was totally amoral, totally insensitive. Were he not, he would never have come back here, never have brought his daughter with him—never have put her in such an invidious position.

By the time Jordan went downstairs again, she had herself in control. She had succeeded in convincing herself that she was behaving foolishly—irrationally— and that the cold sweat which had broken out over her flesh when Karen confirmed that Rhys was back was the natural result of long-suppressed emotions. Rhys had returned to the island; she had to accept that. He had every right to return here. She did not own the island, only a very small part of it—and that, too, was being whittled away by the disturbing decrease in visitors to the hotel. But that was nothing to do with Rhys Williams. That was her affair, her problem; and she had no need of any further problems to trouble her. The most sensible course, so far as Rhys was concerned, was to behave as if the past had never happened, and when they met—as they were bound to do on an island of this size—she would behave with the calmness and dignity won over ten years of self-restraint.

At this time of year the hotel was at its busiest, and she was grateful for that. As she made her way to her office, situated behind the reception desk on the ground floor, she exchanged greetings with several of the guests passing through on their way to change for lunch after a morning spent by the pool. Trade Winds, as her father had christened the hotel, was not a large concern, but it was unique, in that it occupied the finest position on the west coast of the island, and its patrons generally returned for a second, and sometimes a third, visit.

It was approaching noon, and already there was a sense of lethargy creeping over the place. The breezes that usually kept the climate temperate at this time of the year were conspicuous by their absence, and Jordan could feel a trickle of moisture dampening the back of her shirt. Even the wide-legged cotton culottes that covered her slim legs to well below her knees felt uncomfortably sticky, and she refused to associate her present condition with her thoughts earlier. It was a hot day. She was feeling the heat, that was all. And although a visit to one of the many quiet beaches that fringed the island, to swim and sunbathe, was appealing, she was needed here. Besides, she preferred

to keep herself occupied. She would have time enough
to think when the day was over.

The lobby of the hotel was light and airy. A through
draught kept this area cool at all times, and urns of
pampas grass and flowering plants added to its tropical
appearance. There were wickerwork chairs, a small bar
that jutted out below a thatched awning, and rose-pink
quarry tiles underfoot, both functional and attractive.

Jordan's office was small, but functional, too. Here
she discussed menus, answered booking enquiries, and
prepared accounts. There were a dozen other tasks she
did, too, like ordering supplies from the mainland,
choosing colour schemes when the rooms needed
decorating, or arbitrating in disputes between the
other members of the staff. But mostly, her job was
concerned with being available to the guests, to answer
queries and complaints, and to assure herself that
everyone was pulling their weight.

She had a secretary, a local girl called Mary-Jo,
and when she went into her office now, she found the
girl on her hands and knees on the floor. 'Paper-clips,'
Mary-Jo answered her silent enquiry, grimacing as
one of the scattered items dug into an unwary knee.
'Josef's been in here complaining about the shortage of
prawns for tonight's buffet.'

'And he threw these about?' exclaimed Jordan,
joining her on the floor.

'No,' Mary-Jo giggled. 'Not intentionally, that is.
But he did bring his fist down on the desk and the box
just happened to be in the way . . .'

Jordan sighed. 'He really is impossible at times!
And I thought we had enough shellfish.'

'We probably do.' Mary-Jo satisfied herself that she
had collected most of the paper-clips and got to her
feet. 'You know what Josef is like—all bark and no
bite. Here, let me help you.' She gave Jordan her

hand. 'You look worn out.'

'Well, thanks.' Jordan could smile at the backhanded sympathy. 'I am—feeling the heat today. The linen room isn't the coolest place to be when the temperature is in the nineties.'

'You should have let me do it,' exclaimed Mary-Jo, crossing to where a tray was set on a filing cabinet. 'Would you like some orange juice? The ice hasn't melted yet.'

'Please.' Jordan sank down into her own chair behind the desk, and fanned herself with a languid hand. 'Did Karen go down to Mallorys?'

'Yes. She left about a half hour ago,' agreed Mary-Jo, handing over a glass of the sun-tinted fluid. 'There you are—liquid vitamin C!'

Jordan took a taste of the orange juice on to her tongue, savouring its cool sweetness. 'Mmm, delicious,' she murmured, smiling her thanks. 'Just exactly what I needed.'

'Is it?' Mary-Jo looked a little quizzical now, and Jordan's brow furrowed.

'Shouldn't it be?'

'Well——' Mary-Jo paused, 'the way I heard it, something stronger might have been in order. A kind of—stiffener, wouldn't you say?'

Jordan sighed, cradling the glass between her palms. 'You heard,' she said flatly. 'Who told you?'

'I don't remember.' Mary-Jo turned away to pour herself some of the juice. 'Oh, it's all over the island, Jordan. I suppose it was too much to hope that he could come back here without creating a stir.'

Jordan looked down into her glass. 'Well, contrary to public opinion, I don't need a stiffener to face Rhys Williams,' she declared firmly. She looked up at the other girl. 'That was all over long ago, while you were still in school.'

Mary-Jo shrugged. 'You're only five years older than I am, Jordan. I remember what happened at the time. I mean, who wouldn't? Rhys Williams isn't like any ordinary tourist, is he?'

'No.' Jordan's tongue circled her lower lip. 'No, he's not. But there's something else you should remember, Mary-Jo. I was only seventeen at the time, little more than a schoolgirl myself. And that's all it was—a schoolgirl crush on an older man.'

Mary-Jo looked doubtful. 'You were pretty cut up about it when his wife turned up, weren't you?' she protested. 'And who could blame you?'

'Mary-Jo!'

'Well, it's true. I mean, imagine him not telling you he was married! And having a daughter and everything. You must have felt terrible——'

'*Mary-Jo!*'

Jordan's voice had risen sharply, and as if just realising how personal she was being, the girl muttered a word of apology and sat down. But the looks she kept casting in her employer's direction were eloquent of her feelings, and Jordan's nerves felt ragged as she endeavoured to concentrate on the accounts.

She was almost relieved when Karen came back, waltzing into the office with her usual disregard for anyone's privacy. 'The avocados are here!' she announced unnecessarily. And then, with sudden intuition: 'What's been going on here? You could cut the atmosphere with a knife!'

Jordan put down her pen and sighed. 'Mary-Jo and I have just had a difference of opinion,' she declared shortly. 'Now, do you mind if we get on? I seem to have wasted half the day already.'

'All right.' Karen's blue eyes took on a knowing expression. Unlike her sister, she was a natural redhead, and in consequence her colouring was that much fairer. 'But I thought you might like to know, Rhys was in town, with his daughter. At least, I assume she was his daughter. She looks about eighteen.'

'She's—sixteen,' said Jordan slowly, realising, as she did so, how wrong she had been to think of her as a child. Then, colouring, she added: 'Where did you see them? Did you speak to them? I hope you weren't rude—they have as much right here as we do.'

'Hardly,' exclaimed Karen indignantly. 'Daddy's family have lived here for—for donkey's years. And I was born here.'

'I wasn't.'

'No, but you're not like Rhys Williams. He's only lived on the island for a matter of months, not years.' Karen pursed her lips. 'Anyway, you don't have to worry. I didn't speak to them. They didn't even see me, and if they had, I doubt Rhys would have recognised me. I was only ten when he went away.'

Jordan allowed her breath to escape unnoticed. 'You—you could be right. So—where did you see them?'

'In the market.' Karen tucked her hands into the pockets of her shorts. 'He was buying her a sun-hat. One of those hand-made palm things that weigh a ton until they've dried out.' She paused. 'He hasn't changed much.'

'Well, I have.' Jordan tried to make it sound like a joke, but it didn't quite come off. 'I—where did you leave the avocados? Not out in the sun, I hope.'

'No.' Karen gave her an impatient look. 'I'm not stupid. Willy took them down to the cellar.'

'Good.' Jordan managed an approving smile. 'Josef will be pleased anyway.'

She hoped Karen would go now, but her sister

hovered in the doorway, evidently wanting to say something else. Jordan's fingers tightened convulsively round her pen as Karen tried to catch her eye, and she wondered how long her new-found composure would last if it was subjected to these pressures.

'Do you think he'll come here?' Karen asked at last, when it became obvious that her sister was not going to make things easy for her, and Jordan laid down her pen.

'Why should he?'

'To thank you, of course.' Karen hunched her shoulders. 'You have looked after the house for him, haven't you?'

Jordan sighed. 'Tomas and Rosa have looked after the house.'

'Yes, I know. But you know they wouldn't have been as diligent as you have.'

'Oh, Karen!' Jordan drew an unsteady breath. 'Can't we just forget about Rhys Williams? Please? I don't want his thanks, I just want to get on with my life. Now, can I do that?'

Karen's lips compressed. 'Well, I think the whole affair stinks,' she declared rudely, going out of the room and slamming the door behind her, and Jordan was left to face Mary-Jo's knowing gaze as the room resounded with the sound.

The remainder of the morning passed without incident, and during the afternoon Jordan had to contend with other problems about the hotel. The shutter on the window in one of the bathrooms had broken, and she had to summon the carpenter to deal with it. One of the guests had trodden on a sea urchin, and the doctor had to be called to remove the spines. And finally, one of the waiters in the restaurant slipped and sprained his ankle, leaving them short-staffed at the busiest time of the day.

By the time Jordan took her evening shower, she was feeling decidedly frayed at the seams. It had been one of those days, she thought, as she towelled her hair dry before picking up the hand drier to complete the process. Ever since Karen had told her about Rhys Williams, her nerves had been on edge, and she had to force her hand to remain steady as she directed the hot air on to her head.

She was applying a pale gold eye-shadow to her lids when the internal phone rang. 'Mr Ferris is here, Miss Jordan,' Raoul's laconic voice announced in her ear, and she acknowledged the news with an emphatic: 'I'll be right down.'

Thank goodness for Neil, she thought, as she hurried into a raw silk skirt and a full-sleeved blouse. Without his help and encouragement, she might never have succeeded in carrying on after her father died, and his knowledge of the hotel trade had been invaluable. It had been particularly kind of him, considering he owned the only other hotel of any size on the island, and by supporting Trade Winds he had halved the business he could have done. Jordan had known him for years, ever since her father came back to the island, bringing his wife and young daughter with him. But it wasn't until her father died that she learned to appreciate his friendship, and the growing bond of affection that was gradually developing between them.

He was waiting for her in the lobby when she went downstairs, tall and tanned and handsome in his black dinner jacket. He was leaning on the desk, talking to Raoul, who took over the switchboard after Mary-Jo had gone home, and Jordan felt a wave of gratitude sweep over her in his warm familiar presence.

'Hi,' she said, her sandalled feet making little sound

on the tiled floor, and he turned and straightened and came to greet her.

'Hi,' he responded, his hands on her shoulders marvellously reassuring. 'You looked flushed. Have you been hurrying?'

'It has been quite a hectic day,' she conceded, as his lips brushed her cheek. 'Thank goodness you were at the end of it. I can't wait to get away from the hotel for a few hours!'

Neil regarded her intently. 'Really?' He tucked her arm through his. 'Well, don't let's delay. I've got some cocktails cooling over ice, and a fillet of beef cooked with herbs and brandy.'

'Mmm, it sounds delicious,' murmured Jordan, giving Raoul a wave of farewell, and then Neil was tucking her into the front seat of his sleek convertible, and the cares of the day just melted into space.

Unlike Jordan and her sister, Neil did not live in his hotel. He had had a single-storied villa built alongside; adjacent to, and yet separate from, the main buildings. Unlike Trade Winds, the accommodation at Coral Cay was provided in a series of beach bungalows, and in consequence, the area it covered was much greater.

Tonight, Jordan could hear the sounds of a beach barbecue as they neared Coral Cay, and the leaping flames of a fire on the sand gave the night an added illumination. Fortunately, it was cooler now than in the heat of the day, but Jordan had no objections when Neil suggested they had their drinks on the verandah.

Because Coral Cay was at the southernmost point of the island, the view was different from the one Jordan was used to. The sea was not so gentle here; there were breakers splintering over the jagged horns of the reef, and although the bathing was adequate, she much preferred the smoother shores of home.

Neil emerged from the house carrying a flask of

cocktails and setting two glasses down on the glass-topped table beside her chair, he poured the bubbling liquid. 'Daiquiris à la Ferris,' he said teasingly, handing her a wide-lipped glass. 'Just what you need after a tiring day.'

'Is it ever!' murmured Jordan fervently. 'Beautiful! You'd make a good barman, Neil. If you ever need a job, come and see me.'

Neil subsided into the cushioned chair beside her, depositing a kiss at the corner of her mouth before stretching his legs out before him. 'The very best part of the day,' he averred, tasting his own drink. 'So, tell me: why are you so feeling so drained?'

'Oh——' Jordan was glad of the shadows on the verandah to hide her sudden colour. 'You know—this and that. The usual ups and downs of an hotelier's life.'

'And that's all?' Neil turned his head to look at her. 'Just the usual pitch and toss?'

'What else?' Jordan lifted one foot to rub her instep lightly against her leg. In the dark, the whiteness of her skirt was a sharp contrast to the brownness of her skin, and she reflected how lucky she was never to need tights or stockings. 'One of the French girls stood on a sea urchin, and Carlos chose tonight of all nights to go and sprain his ankle.'

'And that was it?'

'Well . . .' Jordan lifted a slim shoulder, feeling the weight of her hair as it coiled against her neck, 'there were one or two other irritations, but yes, I guess that was all.'

'Oh, Jordan!' Neil leant forward to pour more of the pale liquid into his glass. 'You're not telling me you haven't heard that Rhys Williams is back, are you? According to Karen, she virtually ran into him in town today, and I know she wouldn't keep that piece of news to herself.'

Jordan stiffened. 'You've spoken to Karen?'

'Sure. She was in the lobby talking to Raoul when I arrived. As soon as she mentioned Williams' name I guessed how you'd react. Damn the fellow! What's he come back here for?'

Jordan hesitated. 'Rosa told me he was coming for a holiday,' she admitted after a moment, and Neil frowned.

'You knew he was coming, then?'

'Y—e—s.' Jordan drew the word out. 'I—it's not unnatural, is it? I mean, he does own the house at Planter's Point.'

'I don't know how he has the nerve to come here,' snapped Neil angrily. 'But I suppose it's all you can expect from *artists*!' The way he said the word was an abuse. 'I'd have thought he'd have better things to do than come here, raking up old gossip! From the little I've read about him in the American press, he's not been short of female companionship during the past ten years.'

'Neil, please!' Jordan sat up, straightening her spine. 'It's not that important.'

'It's important to me,' retorted Neil grimly. 'I may not have had a personal interest in you at that time, but I know how you must have felt when his wife turned up like that. Everyone thought you were going to marry the fellow, didn't they? No wonder your father didn't approve!'

Jordan sighed. 'Look, can we talk about something else? I appreciate your sympathy, but—well, it's really not necessary. It all happened a long time ago. I was too young to know what I was doing. Let's forget it, shall we? According to Rosa, he's only staying a few weeks. I probably won't even see him.'

CHAPTER THREE

IT was raining. After weeks of unmitigated heat, the weather had finally broken, and the downpour promised to soak Jordan long before she reached home. Already it was difficult to see where she was going, the tropical cloudburst causing giant puddles in the road, and almost blinding her as it swept across the bouncing bonnet of the buggy.

There had been only a hint of what was to come before she left the hotel. A distant rumbling had warned of thunder, but the sky had seemed clear enough. However, the storm clouds from the west had blown up with unexpected force, and now the clouds were leaden and the rain was falling with steady persistence.

Sighing, Jordan pulled the buggy over to the side of the road, ignoring the dangers of the bending trunks above her. There didn't seem much point in scrabbling around in the back of the buggy looking for the storm canopy now. Her face and arms were soaked, as was her hair, and the short skirt of her cotton tunic revealed that her legs were dripping with water, too.

A brief appraisal of her whereabouts informed her that she was only about half a mile from Planter's Point, and in other circumstances she would have had no hesitation in seeking shelter at her father's old home. But having survived Rhys's first week on the island without running into him, she was just beginning to relax, and she had no intention of precipitating a meeting.

Nevertheless, the idea of sitting in the buggy until the storm passed was not attractive to her, and deciding she couldn't get any wetter than she was now, she slid out on to the grass verge. Through the belt of trees she could see the strand of beach, strewn with the debris blown from the trees, and beyond it the sea, rain-washed and inviting.

On impulse, she dropped her sandals into the back of the buggy, and padded across the turf to the sand. The texture of the grass was soft against her toes, stroking her bare legs in a curiously sensuous gesture. The sand, too, was fine and gritty as her feet sank into it, making walking difficult until she reached the damper stretches where the tide had reached.

The soles of her feet made footprints in the sand, but they disappeared almost immediately, absorbed into the springy wetness. And as she approached the sea, creaming in rivulets along the shoreline, the waves took the evidence of her occupation away, rippling round her toes and splashing over her ankles.

Her hair dripped lankly down her neck, and realising it would never dry in its present state, she reached up her arms and pulled out the pins that kept it securely in place. It fell down her back in a long silken curtain, and she ran her fingers through it, enjoying the unaccustomed freedom. Turning her face up to the heavens, she parted her lips and drank in the storm's sweetness, then spread her arms wide in an all-encompassing attitude.

She didn't know at exactly what moment she became aware of the man's presence. It might have been an unconscious realisation in the back of her mind as she lifted her face to the sky. Or it could, conceivably, have been the moment when she spread her arms in that gesture of obeisance and caught sight of the still dark figure silhouetted along the beach.

Immediately, her arms fell to her sides, and she shifted a little uneasily. She felt as if she had been caught out in some flagrant act of abandon, not at all the kind of behaviour expected from the manager of the Trade Winds Hotel. Making an effort to justify her actions, she looped the rain-darkened rope of her hair over one shoulder and squeezed the moisture from it; then, with a careless lift of one shoulder, she started towards the buggy, realising as she did so that the rain was beginning to ease.

The man had started to move, too. She could see him out of the corner of her eye, and although she quickened her step, it was obvious he was going to intercept her before she reached the road. *Damn*, she thought impatiently, why had she decided to stop? This was a deserted stretch of the highway, and although she was not exactly afraid, she couldn't help remembering her own reckless behaviour. Perhaps he thought she was looking for company; she could hardly blame him if he had got the wrong impression. And looking down at her breasts outlined against the thin cotton of her bodice, she knew it would be difficult to convince him otherwise.

With a feeling of frustration, she gave up the unequal struggle to reach the buggy and turned to confront her pursuer. Attack was the only method of defence left to her, she decided, and sweeping back her wind-blown hair she held it in place at her nape with both hands.

'Are you following me?' she began, before her breath caught in her throat, almost choking her. '*Rhys!*' she exclaimed, swallowing convulsively, and then more evenly: 'Rhys! What a surprise! Wh-what are you doing here?'

It was all so much different from the way she had intended their eventual meeting to take place. To begin with, she had expected him to come to the hotel, as Karen had said, to thank her for looking after his house if nothing else. When that didn't happen, she had steeled herself to meeting him every time she went into the little town of Eleutha, but once again, she had not seen him. She had planned their meeting so minutely, even down to the clothes she would wear and the things she would say, but all that was useless now. She had never expected to encounter him on a rain-soaked afternoon, miles from the hotel, with her hair and clothes clinging to her like a second skin, and without a scrap of make-up to disguise the panic that raged inside her.

And he looked just the same—a little older perhaps, but not significantly so, his dark hair plastered to his head, outlining the lean contours of his face and jawline. He was still as attractive as ever, moving with that lithe, cat-like grace, that characterised his sexuality. Like her, his clothes were wet and sticking to him, though he had unbuttoned the denim shirt and it hung loose from his shoulders. Jeans moulded his thighs, but she determinedly kept her eyes on the silver clasp of his belt. She didn't want to look at him, she didn't want to remember what they had once shared; and most of all she didn't want him to look at her, particularly not when his expression clearly mirrored a fine contempt.

'I should ask you that question,' he said now, covering the space between them. 'You're trespassing, or did you know that?' His dark eyes compelled her gaze. 'What the hell did you think you were doing back there?'

Jordan took several deep breaths to calm herself, but without a great deal of success. He was angry, that much was evident, and even being civil was obviously an effort.

Wrapping her arms closely about her, she lifted her head. 'I—I don't know what you mean,' she said carefully. 'I was just killing time until the storm had cleared. I didn't know I was trespassing, but if you say I was, I'll take your word for it.'

'Thanks.' Rhys's features twisted. 'Just tell me something—did you come here deliberately, even after I told Rosa to keep you away?'

'You told Rosa——'

'Making a spectacle of yourself like that, in view of anyone who cared to look! My God, what's happened to you, Jordan? Have you taken up rain worship or something? Or was that little charade for my benefit? You apparently knew I was there.'

'I did not!' Jordan's indignation was her only defence. 'I wasn't doing anything wrong.'

'No?'

'No.' She licked the rainwater from her lips. 'What's it to you anyway? I wouldn't have expected you to be prudish, Rhys.' She paused. 'And I didn't ask you to watch, did I?'

'So you admit you were putting on an act?'

'I do not.' Jordan's dark eyes had taken on the greenish tinge of the sea and they sparkled resentfully. She shook her head. 'I don't have to listen to this, you know. What I do or don't do is my own affair. Now, will you please step out of my way. I'd like to get back to my car.'

'That—vehicle—is yours?'

'The buggy, yes.' Jordan endeavoured to hide the fact that she was trembling. 'Excuse me, I have to get back.'

Rhys didn't move. 'To the hotel?' he enquired tautly, and she nodded. 'What are you doing on this road?'

Jordan gasped. 'That's my business!'

'I'm making it mine.'

She shook her head. 'This is ridiculous! Get out of my way!'

'In a minute.' Rhys stepped closer to her. 'When you've told me what you were doing prowling round my property.'

'Oh, for heaven's sake!' Jordan was feeling distinctly apprehensive now. 'I was not—prowling round your property. As a matter of fact, Nana's ill. I've been to see her.'

'Nana? Oh, your old nurse.'

'That's right.' Jordan suppressed the urge to physically keep him at bay. 'If you remember, she lives at the other side of the island.'

'Oh, I remember.' Rhys wiped an impatient hand along his jaw. 'And that's the only reason you stopped here?'

'I've told you. It's raining, or hadn't you noticed. I couldn't see where I was going.'

Rhys hesitated, then stepped back again, much to her relief. 'All right, I suppose I have to believe you.'

'You can please yourself.' Jordan's words were bravely said, even if her voice was tremulous. 'Now, do you mind if I get on?'

Rhys lifted his shoulders. 'Be my guest.'

'Thank you.'

It was an effort to walk past him to the buggy. She was trembling so much, her limbs seemed incapable of responding to the simplest commands, and she was sure he would notice. Her short skirt and bare legs were terribly revealing, and with the sodden curtain of her hair about her shoulders, she felt as coltish and ungainly as the teenager she had once been.

The seat of the buggy was a puddle of water, but she didn't stop to wipe it away. With quivering fingers, she fired the ignition, and expelled her breath in deep relief when it responded at the first attempt.

The first person she saw when she got back to the hotel was Karen, and her sister regarded her with some concern. 'What happened to you?' she exclaimed. 'Couldn't you have waited until the storm was over to drive home? I know you wanted to make sure the musicians had arrived, but I could have handled it.'

'I know that.' In all honesty, Jordan had forgotten about the planned entertainment for the evening. 'I—it wasn't raining when I left. I thought I'd make it in time.'

'Well, obviously you didn't.' Karen pulled a face. 'But it's quite a change to see you looking your age for once. You look nice with your hair loose, Jordan. I've always thought so.'

Jordan turned away towards the stairs. 'The pins came out,' she offered, unwilling to discuss the reasons for her dishevelment. 'I'm going to take a shower. Send me up some tea, will you, love?'

'Is that necessary? The shower, I mean.'

Karen's amused retort followed her up the stairs, but Jordan made no response. She badly needed to recover her composure and her equilibrium, and restoring her appearance to its usual neatness was the only way she knew to initiate the process.

In her bedroom, however, she viewed her bedraggled state with reluctant compulsion. She wanted to see for herself what Rhys must have seen, and her skin crawled in humiliation at the sorry picture she presented. Hair like rats' tails, clothes sticking to her, long bare legs streaked with mud: she didn't have to look at her face to know she had made a fool of herself. Nevertheless, her eyes did seek their reflection in the mirror, faltering at the tremulous expression they saw there, and moving on over pale cheeks to the vulnerable separation of her mouth. Dear God, she thought, with painful self-derision, what must he have thought of her? After all this time, she should have been more prepared for his censure, but she wasn't. What had she expected? Why had she been so shocked? They were antagonists after all, not acquaintances; enemies, not friends. How could she have anticipated civility from Rhys, when their parting had been so savage?

Two days later, Jordan was returning from an early morning swim when she saw Mary-Jo coming to meet her. Most of the guests were at breakfast, and Jordan had taken the opportunity to relax for a while, away from her hotel duties. Besides which, she had been awake for hours, waiting for the pale golden light of morning to slat through the shutters, and the sand crabs had still been active when she tossed a towelling jacket about her shoulders and made her way down to the lagoon.

Now, seeing Mary-Jo hurrying towards her, she knew an immediate premonition of disaster. What had happened? she wondered. Surely in the hour or so she had been absent no sinister misfortune had taken place. But the ominous feeling persisted, and she quickened her step accordingly.

'I've been looking for you.' Mary-Jo's dark face mirrored her concern. 'You weren't in your room and you weren't on the terrace. I was worried!'

'Worried?' Jordan gave her a disbelieving look. 'I've swum in the morning before. Why didn't you ask Karen where I was?'

'I did, but she said she didn't know.'

'No, but—well—oh, this is ridiculous.' Jordan shook her anxieties aside. 'What is it? Why did you need to find me so urgently? Don't tell me—Mrs Lorrimer has found cockroaches in the bathroom!'

Mary-Jo shook her head. 'It's no joke, Jordan. I just wanted to tell you before you found out for yourself.'

'Found what out?' Jordan couldn't deny the little frisson of apprehension that was making itself felt in the pit of her stomach. 'What has happened that's of such earth-shattering importance you felt the need to come and find me?'

'Rhys Williams has booked a table for dinner tonight,' announced Mary-Jo, somewhat sulkily, evidently deciding her employer's attitude was not worthy of her distress. 'I just thought you'd want to know, that's all. I'm sorry, I didn't think it was amusing.'

Nor did Jordan, and her cheeks hollowed as she sucked in her breath. 'How—how do you know this?' she demanded, struggling to keep her emotions at bay, and Mary-Jo shrugged.

'I read it—this morning. He must have rung last night, when Raoul was in charge of the switchboard. But it's there in black and white, if you don't believe me. A table for two at nine o'clock.'

'I—I believe you.' Jordan tightened the cord of her towelling jacket. Rhys was coming here! He was actually planning to eat dinner at her hotel—with his daughter. What kind of game was he playing?

'I told Karen,' added Mary-Jo, falling into step beside Jordan as she began to walk numbly back to the hotel. 'She said you wouldn't be bothered, but I didn't believe her.'

'What? Oh—oh, yes, you did right to tell me,' murmured Jordan painfully. 'I—just can't imagine why he's coming here.'

'Can't you?' Mary-Jo cast a sceptical look in her direction. 'I can. He wants to see you, of course. He's been on the island over a week now and he's curious. I imagine he expected you to go out to the house. As you haven't, he's coming here.'

Jordan moistened her dry lips. 'That's your assessment, is it?' She had told no one of that brief encounter near Planter's Point, but now she half wished she had. 'Well, I doubt he's coming to see me, Mary-Jo. We didn't exactly—part—on the best of terms.'

'Why do you think he's coming, then?' asked the other girl, as they reached the three shallow steps that led up to the terrace.

To their left, the pool glistened blue-green in the sunlight edged about with cushioned li-los and locally woven garden furniture. To the right, a palm-thatched awning gave protection to the outdoor restaurant, and as Jordan responded to the greetings of the guests seated nearest the steps, she realised she couldn't answer that question either.

'I—oh, I should think he's getting bored with the rustic life,' she said now, hoping Mary-Jo would let the subject drop, but she didn't.

'Why should he be getting bored after only a week?' she exclaimed. 'Last time he was here, he stayed more than six months. He didn't seem to be getting bored then.'

'Perhaps he was more easily entertained in those days,' said Jordan unwillingly as they entered the lobby of the hotel. 'I don't know, do I, Mary-Jo? Now, excuse me: I have to go and get dressed.'

She seemed to spend all her time escaping from awkward conversations these days, Jordan thought frustratedly, as she put on the buttercup yellow wrap-around skirt and matching sleeveless vest she had laid out before going for her swim. And it was all because of Rhys Williams, damn him! Why hadn't he sold the house and stayed in Europe or the United States—where he belonged!

The day passed agonisingly slowly. Every time the phone rang, Jordan tensed, half expecting to hear that Rhys had cancelled his reservation, but no such relief was forthcoming. She would have contacted Neil and invited herself to his house for dinner, but he had flown to the mainland the previous afternoon, and was not expected back until the next day. She had no excuse to be absent, she thought bitterly, and by six o'clock her nerves were shredded.

Karen encapsulated Jordan's own summation of the situation when she said she thought Rhys was bringing his daughter to Trade Winds deliberately. 'He wants you to see her,' she declared frankly, coming into the office where Jordan was unsuccessfully trying to repair the stapling machine. 'And no doubt he's curious about you, too. Who wouldn't be after ten years? I must admit, I got quite a shock myself when I saw him.'

Jordan's head lifted. 'You said—you said he looked much as you remembered.'

'Yes, I did.' Karen draped herself over a corner of the desk and examined her finger nails. 'But I was only a kid when he was last here, remember? I didn't realise how——' she coloured—'well, how attractive he is. I'm sorry, Jordan,' she added awkwardly, 'I realise you'd rather not hear this, but I feel I should warn you. He hasn't lost his—appeal.'

Jordan's lips tightened. 'Thank you.'

'No, I mean it.' Karen shifted her position. 'Honestly, Jordan, that picture we saw of him in the *Woman's Journal* didn't do him justice.'

'Are you a fan?' Jordan's voice was clipped, but at least she succeeded in hiding the pain her sister's words had caused her. What was Karen implying? she wondered uneasily. That she might have made a mistake in breaking with him? Or that Karen herself found him attractive, too? 'I imagine Rhys Williams knows his appeal better than anyone,' she added, unable entirely to suppress the tinge of bitterness. 'After fifteen years of the kind of success he's enjoyed, it would be difficult not to.'

'Oh, Jordan!' Karen stared at her defensively. 'I'm not saying I'd ever get involved with him. It's just that, having seen him, I'm beginning to understand how you must have felt when he started to take an interest in you.'

Jordan drew a deep breath. 'I see.'

'Were you—I mean, did you——?' Karen faltered, and then finished lamely: 'Were you very close?' which was obviously not what she had been going to ask at all. 'You don't talk about it, do you? I only know the bare facts: that you used to spend a lot of time with him when he was here, and that Daddy didn't approve. Then his wife turned up, with the child. That's all I know.'

'That's all there is.' Jordan's voice was crisp. 'Oh, I've told you, I was too young to know better. And like Daddy said, he took advantage of me.'

Karen opened her mouth to ask the obvious question this provoked, then closed it again. Evidently she would have liked to question her sister more closely about her involvement, but discretion—and a certain lack of assurance—caused her to think again. Although, as Jordan was older, Karen had often confided in her, the situation had never been reversed. This particular part of her past was something Jordan had always avoided, and over the years it had been tacitly agreed that that episode was taboo.

Now, however, Jordan sensed Karen's curiosity with some sympathy. Not for the first time, she wished she had someone she could confide in. There had never been anyone, except Nana, who was too old now to burden with her problems. She had sometimes wondered, had her mother been alive, whether she might never have become infatuated with Rhys Williams in the first place. An older woman might have been wary of his interest in her daughter and tactfully defused the situation. Jordan's father had not realised what was happening until it was too late, and by then Jordan was fathoms deep in love with the sophisticated young musician.

In her room later, dressing for the evening, Jordan deliberately chose one of the least attractive outfits in her wardrobe. Her striped navy and white shirt had a round Peter Pan collar, and the narrow sleeves had broad, workmanlike cuffs. With it she wore a plain navy skirt, whose only drawback in her eyes was its shortness, but flat-heeled leather sandals seemed to negate any attention being drawn to her legs. Her hair she plaited into a single braid before skewering it securely on top of her head, thus removing any trace of gentleness it might have given to her features.

It was a quarter to eight when she went downstairs, and in spite of her intention to go straight to her office, she was cornered by two of the guests who wanted to discuss the whereabouts of some caves on the island.

'Maury—that's our friend—stayed here last year, and he was telling us about these fantastic caves you can dive into,' exclaimed Shelley Palmer, a young American who was holidaying with her boy-friend. 'He says they're really worth the trouble, and Jason and I wondered if you knew where we could hire some equipment.'

Jordan offered her polite smile. 'Well, we can arrange the scuba equipment for you,' she agreed. 'But I would advise you to talk to our resident expert first. The caves are worth a visit, but only someone used to deep-water diving should attempt it.'

'Oh, Jason's used to it,' the American girl dismissed her fears airily. 'He works for an oil company. He's done a lot of deep-sea diving, haven't you, darling?'

Jason Ascani looked rueful. 'Some,' he conceded, giving Jordan a reassuring grin. 'But we may take a rain-check on that particular trip, Shelley. Your experience is limited to shallower waters.'

'Hey, don't be a spoilsport!' Shelley pursed her lips. 'You promised you'd give it a try.'

'As I recall it, I said I'd give the matter some thought,' Jason told her firmly. 'And now, we're keeping Miss Lucas from getting on with her job.' He grinned at Jordan. 'Thanks for your help. I'll let you know if we need any further information.'

'You do that,' Jordan nodded, and was just about to make good her escape when it happened. One moment she was following them across the lobby, feeling a little sorry for Shelley as she loudly protested her competence, and the next she had frozen to a standstill. Two people had entered the hotel during their discussion, and were now approaching the reception desk. One was a girl, a teenager, wearing a pale blue cotton jump suit, her streaked blonde hair expertly cut to frame her face like an inverted bell. The other was a man, casually but expensively dressed in narrow-legged black corded pants and a silk shirt of the same sombre shade, a jerkin that matched his slacks looped carelessly over one shoulder.

Rhys! thought Jordan sickly, knowing, without even needing to look at his face that she was not mistaken. She was experiencing an entirely physical reaction to his presence, and every inch of her skin felt raw, as if someone was scraping a sharp knife across her flesh.

It was the moment for decision, she knew. She could ignore them. She could turn and walk into her office without acknowledging either of them, in which case Rhys would form his own assessment of her motives. Or she could go and greet them as she would any other guest of her acquaintance who might come to the hotel for a meal. The choice was hers, and without doubt her actions would be reported afterwards. Submission or resistance, that was what it boiled down to. To be a mouse—or a cat. She chose the latter.

Ignoring the sudden intake of breath from Raoul hovering behind the desk, she pinned a polite smile to her lips and advanced towards them, holding out her hand.

'Rhys!' she exclaimed, with every appearance of total self-possession, as if they had parted ten years ago on the best of terms and not seen one another since. 'How nice of you to remember our small establishment!'

CHAPTER FOUR

RHYS was shocked. Just for a moment, before the mask of urbanity slid down to guard his expression, Jordan saw the sudden wariness that crossed his face and was glad. The brief drawing together of his brows acknowledged her small gesture, then the thin lips parted to reveal the even white teeth she remembered so well. His smile might not reach his eyes, but it was nonetheless disarming in spite of that, and Jordan's nerves tightened in unwelcome awareness. Two days ago, at Planter's Point, she had found him disturbing; tonight he was both disturbing and dangerous, and she could quite see why Karen had felt the need to warn her. The dark clothes accentuated the air of controlled power about him, the golden texture of skin stretched tautly over his bones, so that every movement he made was sinuously defined. Eyes the colour of dark honey, regarded her with penetrating thoroughness, stripping her attempt at sophistication aside, and discarding it. She was ensnared, pinioned by the raw contempt she saw lurking in his eyes, and her courage faltered. He hadn't changed at all, she thought unsteadily. How could she have imagined she could control this situation, when she couldn't even control herself?

'Not such a small establishment,' he remarked now, as his long fingers curled briefly round hers, and for a moment she didn't know what he was talking about. But then recollection dawned and, aware that the girl beside him was watching her with narrowed eyes, she made an effort to regain her composure.

Withdrawing her hand from his, she folded it inside

her palm, ignoring the tingling sensation that had run up her arm at the contact. 'Smaller than you're used to,' she countered, forcing a tight smile to her lips. 'This—this must be your—daughter.'

The girl tucked her hand possessively through her father's arm, regarding Jordan without liking. Evidently she was used to enjoying Rhys's undivided attention, and her lower lip jutted petulantly as she said: 'Can we get a drink, Daddy?'

Ignoring her plea, Rhys inclined his head. 'Yes,' he said smoothly. 'This is Lucy. Lucy, this is an old— friend of mine: Jordan Lucas.'

'Hi.' Lucy's reluctant acknowledgement was accompanied by a languid lifting of her hand, then she turned to her father again. 'I'm thirsty, Daddy. Can I have a Bacardi and Coke?'

'Shortly,' said Rhys, with an edge to his tone, and Jordan was taken aback. She had expected him to tell her she was too young to drink alcohol, but after all, she reminded herself bitterly, Rhys Williams adhered to no one's rules but his own.

'I want to talk to you, Jordan,' he said instead, glancing half impatiently about him, and her pulse palpitated wildly. 'Is there some place Lucy can go while we have a few words?'

'I——'

Jordan was desperately trying to think of some excuse for refusing when his daughter intervened. 'Why can't I stay with you, Daddy?' she protested. 'I won't get in the way.' She gave Jordan a sidelong glance that possessed the kind of maturity Jordan herself would find difficult to emulate even now, and lifted one tanned shoulder. 'Whatever you have to say to—Miss Lucas, I don't mind.'

'No, Lucy.' Rhys accompanied the terse denial with a taut smile. Then to Jordan: 'Where's Karen? She's still here, isn't she? Perhaps she'd look after Lucy while we talk.'

'Oh, really, Rhys——' Jordan glanced round unhappily, and as she did so, she saw Karen watching them, half concealed behind the climbing plants that covered a bamboo trellis. 'I—here's Karen now.' She beckoned her sister forward with an imperative gesture. 'Look, Karen will answer all your questions. I can't stop and chat. I've got work to do.'

Karen came forward eagerly, and Jordan saw with some frustration that her sister was wearing one of her most attractive outfits. Her dress of dark blue taffeta had a strapless boned bodice, and with her red-gold curls framing her face like an aura, she looked almost beautiful. 'Hello, Rhys,' she said, the breathy quality of her voice not lost on his daughter. 'How nice to see you again.'

Jordan's eyes sought the roof in a momentary supplication, then she impaled her sister with a baleful stare. 'You'll show——Mr and Miss Williams to the bar, won't you, Karen?' she directed sharply, and the other girl's nod of acquiescence did nothing to reassure her.

Rhys however was not so easily dismissed. 'I'm sure you can spare me five minutes, Jordan,' he declared, detaching himself from his daughter's clinging hands and pushing her gently, but firmly, in Karen's direction. 'You'll look after Lucy, won't you, Karen? You know,' he gave her an admiring look, 'you're not a bit like the pigtailed schoolgirl I remember.'

Karen coloured with pleasure, and only Lucy, apart from Jordan herself, seemed to find anything to object to in the arrangements. 'But, Daddy——' she began, evidently about to complain, and he pulled a roll of dollar bills out of his pocket.

'Buy Karen a drink, sweetheart,' he said, pushing them into her hand, and Lucy took the notes resignedly and made no further protest.

As the two girls walked away, Rhys swung his jacket off his shoulder and regarded Jordan questioningly. 'The office is back there, isn't it?' he enquired tersely, gesturing towards the reception desk. 'We can use that.'

'For what?' Jordan drew an unsteady breath. 'Rhys, I think anything we have to say to one another can be said right here. I don't know what game you think you're playing, but I won't be a party to it.'

'Game? Who said anything about a game?' responded Rhys, his hand at her elbow compelling her forward. 'Now, you don't want to cause a scene, do you?'

Jordan wrenched her arm out of his grasp, and realising that by giving in to her emotions she was playing into his hands, she quickened her step to put several paces between them. As luck would have it, Raoul had been called away from the reception desk at that moment, and her silent appeal that he might need her assistance was doomed to disappointment. It seemed she was obliged to face this interview after all, and her heart was beating rapidly as Rhys closed the door behind them.

For several seconds he didn't speak; he simply took a note of his surroundings, then nodded his head as if they were exactly as he remembered them. Then, tossing the jerkin on to the metal filing cabinet by the door, he gave his attention to her.

'What the hell have you got your hair screwed up like that for?' he demanded, massaging the muscles at the back of his neck. 'I liked it better the way you had it the other day, even if it was wet and sticking to you.'

Jordan stiffened. 'Is that what you wanted to talk about? My hair?'

'I imagine this—outfit—is for my benefit, is it?' he remarked carelessly. 'The no-nonsense skirt and the schoolmarmish blouse. What a pity you didn't wear trousers—that would have completed the image.'

'What do you mean?' Jordan caught her breath.

'I mean you're trying to disguise your femininity, aren't you?' he retorted harshly, moving about the room. He flicked his thumb through the pile of invoices scattered over her desk, his lips twisting sardonically. 'It's a blind, isn't it? The unsubtle image of the butch hotel proprietor!'

'No!' Jordan quivered with indignation. 'Just because I don't dress to satisfy your doubtful sensibilities, it doesn't mean I'm trying to deny my sex! How dare you say so? You know nothing about me.'

'Not now, perhaps,' he agreed, with a careless shrug. 'But you didn't use to be so—severe.'

'Do you mean ten years ago?' Jordan's voice had risen a little in spite of her resolve. 'I was a child then, Rhys. Or had you forgotten that?'

'I hadn't forgotten.' He had halted a few feet from her and was now standing regarding her with nerve-racking intensity. 'Nevertheless, I can't help associating your appearance with the fact that I rang and booked a table for dinner this evening.'

'That's your prerogative.'

'Yes, it is.' His hand ran almost absently down his throat, his fingers finding and lingering on the fine gold chain suspended there. 'I could have arrived without warning, you know. I wonder how you'd have reacted then?'

Jordan held up her head. 'What do you mean—how I'd have reacted? I haven't—reacted—at all. I would just like to know what makes you think you have the right to come here and catechise me? You're a guest in the hotel, and as such you have certain privileges. But they do not include forcing your way in here and insulting me!'

'I'm not insulting you, dammit!' he swore angrily. 'Dear God, I'm just trying to get a little human response from you! You should know what's happened to you, for heaven's sake!'

'Nothing's happened to me——'

'Hasn't it, by God!' Rhys pushed back his hair with frustrated fingers. 'Oh, what the hell! Why should I care? I didn't come here to get involved in an argument over semantics.'

'Why did you come here?' she demanded fiercely. 'I should have thought after the way you behaved the other day this was the last place you'd want to visit.'

'Why? Because I ordered you off my land?' Rhys rolled his eyes heavenward. 'I was angry then, sure. But it wasn't just because you were trespassing.'

'No?'

'No.' He inhaled deeply. 'Look, this isn't getting us anywhere.' He expelled his breath again heavily. 'Let's start again, shall we? And I'll tell you why I really came.'

Jordan took a backward step and came up against Mary-Jo's desk. He was too close. She didn't feel she could breathe. And it wasn't easy to continue with this when every nerve in her body was sensitised to the subtle sexuality he exuded.

'I—is this necessary——' she began, only to be overruled when Rhys countered harshly: 'Yes, it is!'

He pushed his hands into the back hip pockets of his pants, tautening the cloth across his thighs with unconscious arrogance. 'I wanted to apologise. Yes——' this as she opened her mouth to protest—'I came here to try and make peace between us, not to start another war. Okay, I know I was bloody savage the other day, but I felt savage, and finding you there, on my stretch of beach—well, I guess I just saw red.'

'*You* saw red!'

'Look, stop trying to score points, will you?' He made an impatient gesture. 'I know this may be difficult for you to believe, but when I saw you, I realised I didn't hate you any more——'

'*You—hated—me?*'

Jordan almost choked on the words, and she saw the perceptible thinning of his lips as he struggled to control his temper. 'Yes,' he said grimly. 'Yes, I hated you. Did you expect my gratitude for walking out on me like that?'

'And did you expect me to stay around and *share* you with your wife?' spat Jordan scornfully. 'My God! What do you take me for?'

Rhys closed his eyes for a moment and then opened them again. 'This is getting us nowhere,' he said, in a clipped, expressionless tone. 'Can't you stop bitching long enough to listen to what I have to say, or are you so eaten up with your own importance you don't think anyone else has a right to a hearing?'

Jordan gasped. 'I didn't ask you to come here.'

'No, you didn't,' he agreed wearily. 'But I'm here now, and the least you can do is give me an audience.'

Jordan was trembling so much she could hardly stand still, and turning her back on him, she wrapped her arms closely about herself. 'I want you to go,' she said huskily. 'I don't want to listen to your excuses. I don't even want to see you. Please—leave me alone!'

The word he used then was one Jordan hardly understood, but its meaning was clear. With a violent gesture, he snatched his jerkin off the filing cabinet and flung open the door, slamming it behind him with such force that the flimsy partition between the office and the lobby was shaken to its foundations.

Karen found her about ten minutes later.

'They've gone!' she announced blankly, closing the office door behind her so that Raoul, who was now at the desk, should not hear what she was saying. 'Rhys just came across to the bar and yanked Lucy up out of her seat and said 'We've leaving!' She didn't argue. Not that I'd have argued with him in that mood—hey! What happened?'

'Nothing.' Jordan had been sitting at her desk with her face buried in her hands, but now she turned her head aside, rubbing furiously at her cheeks with fingers that shook abominably. 'It's just—reaction, I suppose. I guess I'm not as tough as I thought I was.'

Karen shook her head. 'But what did he say? And why aren't they staying for dinner? Did you ask them to leave?'

'No.' Jordan pulled a tissue out of the box on her desk and blew her nose furiously. 'At least, not directly.' She sniffed. 'I suppose Rhys decided this place wasn't good enough for them, after all. Does it matter? I'm glad they've gone. We don't want them here.'

Karen shook her head. 'So why are you so upset? Was he very angry?'

'Yes. No. Oh, it wasn't that he was angry, Karen.' Jordan got up from her seat, shredding the tissue between her fingers. 'Look, I'd rather not talk about it. Do you mind? It's over now. I'd like to forget Rhys Williams ever existed.'

Karen sighed. 'Well, I don't understand why he came in the first place,' she declared. 'I mean, if all he intended to do was blow you up, why didn't he keep away?'

'He didn't intend to—to blow me up, as you put it,' said Jordan reluctantly. 'As a matter of fact—as a matter of fact, he came to—to apologise——'

'*To apologise!*' echoed Karen disbelievingly, and her sister nodded.

'Yes.'

'So why are you crying?'

'I'm not crying.'

'You have been. Your cheeks are all puffy, and your eyes are red.'

'Oh, Karen!' sighed Jordan.

'Well, it's true. Look at yourself.' She extracted a mirror from the clutch bag she was carrying and thrust it into Jordan's hand. 'Now tell me he only apologised! Honestly, I wasn't born yesterday.'

Jordan examined her reflection critically, touching the swollen hollows below her eyes with some impatience. Karen was right. She couldn't disguise what had been happening. And why should she pretend when Karen had evidently guessed the truth?

'Oh——' she handed back the mirror rather defeatedly, 'all right, he did upset me. But not over coming here for dinner.'

'What, then?'

Jordan lifted her slim shoulders. 'He thought I looked a fright and said so.'

'Is that all?' Karen grimaced. 'I could have told you that.'

Jordan gave her a wounded look. 'What wrong with what I'm wearing?' she exclaimed defensively.

'There's nothing wrong with what you're wearing,' retorted Karen shortly. 'Except that it doesn't suit you, that's all. And while we're on the subject, what on earth have you done with your hair?'

Jordan reached for another tissue and wiped her nose before replying. 'I don't see what my appearance has to do with Rhys Williams!' she declared painfully. 'Anyway, he's gone now, that's what matters.'

'And that's all he said?'

Jordan hesitated, then she sighed. 'No,' she admitted slowly. 'He—oh, he came here to tell me he didn't hate me any more.'

'*He* didn't *hate* you?' Karen gave a short laugh. 'Why should he hate you?'

'That's what I said.' Jordan moistened her lips. 'I mean, what was I supposed to do? Ignore the fact that his wife was on the island? Still go on seeing him when his six-year-old daughter didn't even recognise him?'

'She didn't?' Karen was listening avidly. 'You mean, he'd walked out on his wife while she was expecting his child?'

Realising that to her sister this was hot gossip, Jordan brought the conversation to an end. 'I don't know the details of their relationship,' she replied briefly. 'And I don't want to know.' She blew her nose for the last time and cleared her throat. 'And now, I think it's time we attended to our other guests, don't you? I'll just run upstairs and repair my make-up. Then I'll join you.'

But once she reached the sanctuary of her apartments, Jordan was in no hurry to go back downstairs. Instead, she pushed open the louvred doors which led on to her balcony, and stepped out into the velvet darkness.

Her apartments were situated at the back of the hotel. All the guests' rooms overlooked the beach, but Jordan's view was confined to the verdant golf course, that angled away to her right, and the lush interior of the island, with its cultivated fields of banana plants and sugar cane. At night, of course, she could only see the floodlit forecourt of the hotel, but the scents of the garden remained, and they drifted up in sweet profusion.

Sighing now, Jordan seated herself in the fan-backed bamboo rocker which had once belonged to her grandmother, and allowed its gentle rhythm to soothe her ruffled senses. Even with the occasional sound of a strident voice to disturb her, she felt at peace here, and gradually the painful scene with Rhys receded into her subconscious.

For more than ten years she had dreaded the thought that some day he might come back. Not consciously perhaps, but it had always been there in the back of her mind, and so long as the house at Planter's Point hadn't been sold, she had known there was a possibility.

And now he had, and the confrontation she had known would come was over. So why did she feel so drained suddenly? So empty of emotion that it was like a physical ache inside her? She had nothing to reproach herself for. Ten years of nurturing her hatred towards him could not be dispelled in one night.

Nevertheless, she was aware that things had not gone the way she could have wished, and her own contribution to the explosion of his anger was not to be admired. Did he now believe she was so embittered she couldn't conduct a civil conversation with him? Had her resentful words revealed the depth of the hurt he had inflicted? She had wanted to appear polite, but indifferent, to meet his uncertain temper with coolness and detachment. She had wanted to convince him that she at least had not let him spoil her life. Instead, she had played right into his hands; she had allowed his arrogant words to get under her skin, and he had no doubt gone away with the picture of a shrewish, frustrated old maid.

She uttered a small groan, despising herself for giving way like that. Why couldn't she have listened to what he had to say, and ignored it? She didn't care what he thought of her, so why had she acted as if she did? She had had ten years to learn self-control, and in the space of a few minutes he had proved her incompetence. And the idea that right now he might be discussing her behaviour with his daughter—maybe even laughing about it—filled her with angry resentment.

Dear God, all she had had to do was keep in mind the ugly scenes that had erupted when his wife put in her appearance all those years ago. If she needed any emotional support, she had only to think of the way he had abandoned Jennifer when she was expecting their child. How he had kept out of her way, refusing to pay her even the statutory maintenance, when he himself was rapidly becoming a millionaire.

He was totally unfeeling and selfish, using her as he had used Jennifer, taking what he wanted and caring nothing for the cost to either of them. Poor Jennifer! She had not lived long after her fateful visit to the island. But her death had saved Jordan from ultimate humiliation, although Jordan herself had not appreciated it at the time . . .

CHAPTER FIVE

JORDAN was a few days past her seventeenth birthday when Rhys Williams first came to Eleutha.

His proposed arrival had been talked about for weeks, of course. It wasn't every day that someone as famous as Rhys Williams visited the islands, let alone bought a house there, and Jordan was as excited as the rest of the population that he had chosen to come and live here.

She was more intimately involved, too. It was her grandparents' home that he was buying, and although she had never lived at the house at Planter's Point, she had often stayed there when she was little. Her father had been born and brought up on the island, although he had been educated in England and had met and fallen in love with his wife there. Jordan herself had been born in London, where her father had worked for the Government. But when her grandfather fell ill, Robert Lucas had come back to the island, and had subsequently bought the Trade Winds Hotel, when the previous owners had put it on the market.

Jordan's mother had been less enthusiastic about living on Eleutha, and after Karen was born she had divided her time almost equally between Eleutha and London. It was no surprise to any of them when she asked her husband for a divorce, but Robert Lucas did become embittered after she married again. However, she and her new husband were killed only a few months later, in a plane crash on the Continent, and in consequence Karen and her father had turned to Jordan for the female affection they missed.

At the time Rhys came to the island, Jordan's father
was badly in need of financial assistance. The hotel
was getting run-down, owing to the absence of capital
needed for renovations, and the sale of the old Lucas
house was going to provide the necessary cash. Besides
which, Jordan's grandparents had both been dead for
a number of years, and like the hotel, the house at
Planter's Point was being neglected. Rhys's arrival had
been both expedient and opportune, and all the
tradespeople on the island had benefited from his
willingness to use local labour, and to spend money.

Jordan's first meeting with Rhys occurred in her
father's company. The day after his arrival he had
called at the hotel for a drink, and to meet Robert
Lucas in person, and Jordan had come up from the
beach, where she had been playing with Karen, to
find her father and his guest enjoying a beer on the
terrace.

Jordan's first reaction had been one of embarrassment, particularly when her father called her over and
introduced them, treating her with the usual mixture
of paternal pride and affection he had always displayed
towards her. He didn't treat her as a child exactly, but
he didn't treat her as an adult either, and Jordan, hot
and flushed at the unexpected encounter, was
supremely conscious of her tangled hair and sandy
legs, and out-of-date bikini.

Later, Rhys had told her, in one of their more
intimate moments, that he had fallen in love with her
there and then, but all Jordan had felt was hot
confusion. The disturbing young man seated on the
terrace beside her father filled her with a variety of
emotions, none of them comforting, and his curious
amber eyes seemed to see right through her agitation.

But it wasn't just his eyes that disturbed her.
Although he had risen politely at her approach, her

father's failure to do so had caused him to lower his lean body back on to the chair, and now he lounged there lazily, apparently indifferent to the sexuality of tight-fitting jeans and a short-sleeved knitted cotton shirt, unlaced across the hair-roughened skin of his chest. His hair was dark and longer than on any other man of her acquaintance, but it looked crisp and vital, owing nothing to the ministrations of artifical conditioners. His face was lean and intelligent, his nose prominent, his mouth thin-lipped, yet sensual. Altogether a fascinating individual, and Jordan remembered how her pulse had raced when her father bade her join them.

'My elder daughter, Jordan,' he said, holding her within the circle of his arm, preventing her escape. 'This is Mr Williams, my dear. He moved into the house at Planter's Point yesterday, and he's just called to make our acquaintance.'

'How do you do, Mr Williams.'

Jordan didn't offer her hand. It was too grubby, and besides, she had the feeling Rhys Williams didn't expect it. He wasn't like the Hammonds or the Ferrises, or any of the other people who visited the island. He hadn't been born to wealth or privilege like some of the families who wintered on Eleutha. She knew that from the publicity handouts that were circulated when his band visited America a couple of years ago. He came from some obscure town in the north-east of England and it was the success of his music that had placed him firmly in the upper income bracket. Besides, he had the understated approach of someone who had grown bored with too much adulation, and although he was polite, Jordan thought he found her father rather pompous.

'I've just been telling Mr Williams, we don't have any of his records here,' remarked Robert Lucas tactlessly. 'I suppose we're out of touch with current trends, but then I never liked rock-an'-roll myself.

Jordan cringed at her father's patronising tone, but Rhys only gave a small smile and didn't correct him. It was left to her therefore to recover the situation, and edging out of her father's embrace, she said: 'Mr Williams doesn't play rock-an'-roll, Daddy. His music is—different. More modern. Like the Beatles.'

'How would you know, Jordan?' Her father's chuckle was somehow belittling, and forgetting where she was for a moment, she lost her temper.

'We do have a radio, Daddy!' she exclaimed. 'And from time to time I do read the newspapers. If you paid more attention to what young people wanted, we might get more guests staying here. They don't want a palm court orchestra any more, you know. They want organs and guitars, and music they can *dance* to!'

Of course, she had to apologise later. After Rhys Williams had departed, her father sent for her, and she was obliged to admit that she had behaved quite unforgivably.

'Not that Williams will have noticed, of course,' said Robert Lucas pedantically. 'The man's a Philistine when it comes to manners or good taste. He had the nerve to ask me if I thought anyone would object if he built a sound studio here on the island. To produce records! Just imagine the kind of people we'd have coming here if that happened.'

Jordan moistened her lips. 'So what did you tell him?'

'I told him that I didn't think he'd get planning permission.' He paused. 'I also told him that I couldn't support him in any such venture, and that in fact I'd actively oppose him if he went ahead with his plans.'

'But, Daddy . . .' Jordan sought for the right words, 'a project like that could create a lot of new jobs——'

'—and destroy a lot of old ones,' inserted her father shortly. 'Good heavens, I'm already beginning to wish I'd never agreed to let Williams buy into the community. I had no idea he had any such plan in mind.'

It was a further two weeks before Jordan saw Rhys again. Working for her father at the hotel kept her busy, and she had been given the distinct impression that any further contact with their new neighbour would not be encouraged. Besides, Rhys's house was some miles along the coast, and it was very rarely her father allowed her to drive the small Volkswagen he himself used.

One afternoon, however, while her father was resting, Rhys himself arrived at the hotel. Dressed in a pair of old denims, cut off just above his knee, and a sleeveless sweat shirt, he looked sun-brown and healthy, the city pallor he had sported when he first came to the island replaced by a smooth golden tan.

Jordan was perched on the stool behind the reception desk, bare feet coiled around the stem, engrossed in the pages of a romantic novel. At this hour of the afternoon, there was little doing, and as the hotel was by no means full at the moment, it was the ideal time for relaxation.

'Mr Williams!' she exclaimed, when his shadow falling across her book caused her to look up, and his lips twisted at the formal salutation.

'Rhys,' he amended, glancing carelessly about him. 'Is your father around? I'd like to speak to him.'

'He's resting at the moment.' Jordan pushed the straps of her thin cotton vest up on to her shoulders again. 'Er—can I help you? Is something wrong?'

Rhys came to the desk and rested his palms upon it, causing her to draw back almost automatically. 'You could say that,' he conceded, his lazy eyes running shamelessly over her face and shoulders and the burgeoning fullness of her breasts. 'My housekeeper's just walked out on me. I wondered if your father might know of someone else who would take the job.'

Jordan's tongue circled her upper lip. 'You're talking about Ruby Skinner, aren't you?' she murmured, trying to ignore the heated scent of his body that was drifting to her nostrils. 'She was your housekeeper, wasn't she?'

'Ruby—yes, that's right. Do you know her?' He grimaced. 'I must admit she didn't strike me as the kind of female your father would employ.'

'Oh, he wouldn't—I mean, he didn't.' Jordan's cheeks went pink as she tried to explain. 'When— when my grandparents owned the house, they employed a married couple, Tomas and Rosalie Simms. They were dismissed after my grandmother died a few years ago, and Daddy closed up the house.'

'I see.' Rhys's tawny eyes were intent. 'And Ruby?'

Jordan's colour deepened. 'When she discovered you'd be needing some help, she persuaded Daddy to give her the job.' She caught her lower lip between her teeth. 'Did she—I mean—did you have some complaint about her?'

Rhys's mouth turned down. 'Don't you know?'

Jordan shifted uncomfortably on her perch. 'Well, she has been known to be—unreliable.'

'Really?' Rhys inclined his head. 'Well, unreliability was not why I kicked her out.'

Jordan sighed, looking down at her book and quickly closing the pages. 'I suppose I could ask Daddy if he knows of anyone else,' she said. 'But I don't like to wake him . . .'

'What about the Simms?' asked Rhys flatly. 'The married couple you mentioned, who used to work for your grandparents. Are they still on the island? Do you think they might come back?'

Jordan looked up. 'They might. The last I heard, Tomas was working for the cane company, but I know he much preferred to be his own boss, so to speak.'

Rhys nodded. 'So where do they live? How can I get in touch with them?'

She hesitated. 'As far as I know, they're living in town, with Rosa's parents.' She paused. 'I could give you their address.'

He straightened away from the desk. 'Couldn't you show me? I don't know Eleutha very well, and I've got the jeep outside.'

Jordan's mouth went dry. 'I'm supposed to be in charge of the desk,' she demurred.

Rhys shrugged. 'There doesn't seem to be much going on at present.' He flicked over the pages of her book. 'Surely you can leave for half an hour. It isn't far into town, is it?'

'About fifteen minutes,' Jordan conceded, excitement rising inside her.

'So?' His eyes were on hers, warm and compelling. 'Come on. You'll be quite safe with me, I promise.' He grinned. 'Ask Ruby!'

Jordan slid down off her stool, gazing at him in horrified fascination. 'You mean—she—she——'

Rhys nodded. 'I guess your father thought I'd appreciate the service,' he remarked dryly. 'Unfortunately, I prefer to do my own hunting.' His eyes assessed the brief cuffs of her shorts as he spoke and Jordan's heart pounded. 'Let's go. Before he wakes up and decides I may have an unhealthy interest in his daughter!'

Thirty minutes later, they were driving back to the hotel after a satisfactory interview with Rosalie. Speaking for herself and her husband, she had confessed that they had been hurt when Mr Lucas offered the position to Ruby Skinner and not to them, and it was soon evident that Rosalie's opinion matched Rhys's own.

'She's no housekeeper, Mr Williams,' she declared fiercely. 'Ain' no one will employ her. Not on a permanent basis, that is,' she added, with an awkward glance at Jordan. 'If you know what I mean.'

'Oh, I think we understand you,' drawled Rhys politely, but Jordan could hear the amusement lurking in his voice, and it was all she could do to keep her face straight.

Back in the jeep again, Rhys was suitably grateful, and Jordan moved her shoulders in a gesture of dismissal. 'It was nothing,' she exclaimed. 'I'm happy for Tomas and Rosa. They loved living at Planter's Point.'

'Even so,' Rhys was persistent, 'I doubt whether your father would have put me on to them.' He grimaced. 'I get the feeling he wishes he'd never sold me the house, and if he could get rid of me by pushing another—well, by pushing someone else like Ruby on to me, he would.'

Jordan sighed. 'He's just old-fashioned, that's all. It takes him some time to come to terms with—with change.'

'Does he ever?' Rhys sounded sceptical, then he shook his head. 'No, don't answer that. It's nothing to do with me. I guess you think I'm pretty ignorant, accepting your help and then criticising your old man.'

'Well, I don't think he'd like being called that,' Jordan conceded ruefully. 'Is that what you call your father?'

'I don't have a father,' said Rhys carelessly. 'I never knew my parents. I was brought up in a series of council homes until I was thirteen. Then I was fostered with a family in Hexham, and I stayed with them until I was old enough to earn my living.'

Jordan turned her head to stare at him. 'But surely—your mother——'

'She abandoned me when I was a few months old. They told me later she was only a kid herself, and I guess she couldn't afford to keep me.'

'Oh, that's awful!'

Jordan was appalled, but Rhys's expression revealed his indifference. 'It's no big thing,' he declared. 'What you never have, you never miss. Isn't that what they say?'

She shook her head. 'Haven't you ever felt curious about your parents? I mean, did you ever try to find out who they were?'

'You're a romantic, Jordan,' he told her gently. 'Do you have any idea how many babies are abandoned every year? My mother never left her name. What chance would I have of tracing her in a population of over fifty million people?'

Jordan bent her head. 'I never thought of that.'

'I've had twenty-six years to think of it,' he responded huskily. 'Don't look like that. It's not important, honestly.' With a lift of his shoulders, he pulled the jeep on to the verge at the side of the road and switched off the engine. 'Tell me about you instead. How long have you lived on Eleutha?'

'Twelve years.' Jordan shifted nervously. 'I think we ought to go on. I promised Raoul I'd be back by four and it's after that now.'

'Can't he wait?' Rhys grimaced. 'I hoped we'd have some time to talk.' He glanced across the road to where the grass gave way to pure white sand. 'Let's go for a walk along the beach. The water is perfect at this time of the afternoon.'

She hesitated. 'A walk?' she ventured, and he nodded.

'Just a walk,' he agreed, lifting his hands, palms towards her. 'Please!'

Jordan drew a deep breath, and then, giving in to a purely emotional impulse, she pushed open her door and got out. 'Fifteen minutes,' she said firmly, and Rhys grinned.

'You really live by the clock, don't you?' he mocked, and her face deepened with becoming colour.

She left the sandals she had donned to come into town in the jeep, noticing as she did so that Rhys followed her example. Then they crossed the dusty track and descended the shallow slope to the beach. At this hour of the day the sand was just pleasantly warm, unlike earlier when it would have burned their feet. The air was balmy, not yet humid, but sufficiently moist to bring a wave of perspiration out on her skin, and Jordan was glad she had not bothered to change.

'This is some place,' said Rhys wryly, fitting his longer stride to hers. He looked down at her with lazily admiring eyes. 'I guess you love it.'

'Mmm.' Jordan felt a curious fluttery feeling in her stomach when he looked at her like that. 'It's my home.'

'Yes.' Rhys led their steps towards the shoreline, treading into the soft waves that surged in constant motion on to the sand. 'You're lucky.'

'My mother didn't think so.' She allowed the silky water to curl about her toes. 'She divorced my father and went back to London. That's where I was born,' she added. 'My sister Karen was born here, on the island.'

'Karen? Oh, the kid.' Rhys nodded. 'You were playing with her, weren't you? The day I came to see your father.'

'That's right.' Jordan wondered why she was able to talk to him so easily. 'My mother never wanted to come here, you see. She was happy in England. All her friends were there.'

'Did she marry again?'

'She did. But she and my stepfather were killed in a plane crash soon afterwards. Daddy was pretty cut up about it.'

'I can imagine.' Rhys turned to look at her. 'Was she like you?'

'Some people said so.' Jordan shrugged. 'I don't know. I don't think I could have done what she did.'

'What? Left your father?'

'That, too. But leaving her children——' She flushed at the realisation of what she was saying. 'I—like your mother, I suppose.'

Rhys's grin was sympathetic. 'Not like my mother,' he assured her dryly. 'But I guess it's something we have in common, hmm?'

His smile was disturbing, and Jordan pushed her hands into the pockets of her shorts and quickened her step. She wondered what his fans would say if they could see her now. No one, seeing them together, would ever suspect he was the 'pop' idol who evoked such hysteria at his concerts. He looked like any other tourist, holidaying on the island, and only when she encountered the smouldering brilliance of his eyes did she understand a little of the excitement his musical genius provoked.

'Slow down,' he said, his hand descending on her shoulder to retard her progress, and she quivered beneath the touch of those long sensitive fingers. 'Hey, are you cold?'

'Cold?' Jordan's skin felt as if it was on fire. 'No, I'm not cold,' she said hurriedly. 'Do—do you think you're going to like it here?'

'Apart from Ruby, you mean?' he countered teasingly, dropping his hand, and Jordan expelled her breath with some relief. 'I think so. I can work here, and that's important to me. I like—most of the people.

I like the climate. And I like my house—your grandfather's house,' he acceded, with a shrug.

'It's your house now,' said Jordan quickly. 'I used to love that place when I was a kid. But after Daddy shut the place up, I never went back.'

'You should.' Rhys had halted, and she was obliged to stop, too, or appear rude. 'I'd like you to see what I've done with it. Oh, nothing radical,' he assured her laughingly, as she lifted anxious eyes to his face. 'Just a coat of paint here and there, and some new furniture. All in keeping with the character of the place, I promise.'

Jordan dragged her gaze away. 'Yes,' she said tautly. 'Yes, I'd like to see it some time. Thank you.'

'When?'

'When?' She shifted in some confusion, keeping her eyes on the distant horizon, realising her father was unlikely to give her permission. 'Oh—I don't know. When you're properly settled in, I suppose.'

'I am "properly settled in",' he countered dryly. 'What's the matter? Don't you think your old man will let you come?'

Jordan looked down at her toes. 'I think—it's unlikely,' she conceded truthfully. 'Daddy doesn't approve of me spending time alone with—with men.'

'Don't you mean with *boys*?' suggested Rhys shrewdly. 'I can't imagine your father foreseeing any possibility of you spending time alone with a man. And I am a man, Jordan, not a boy.'

'I know that.' Jordan hunched her shoulders. 'Like I said, he's old-fashioned.'

'And you're not?'

His eyes mocked her, and she coloured again. 'Probably,' she mumbled. 'Anyway,' she looked back along the beach, 'we ought to be retracing our steps.'

'In a minute.' His fingers encircled her arm just

above her wrist, pulling her hand out of her pocket and turning her to face him. 'Are you afraid of me?'

'Well—I wasn't,' she murmured uneasily, and his lips parted in reluctant amusement.'

'You don't have to be,' he told her softly. 'I only want us to be friends. Dig?'

'Dig?' Jordan was confused, and Rhys's laughter was low and irresistible.

'Understand,' he explained sobering. 'It's an expression, that's all. Like—like saying you're getting high, when what you really mean is you're drunk. Slang, I suppose your father would call it.'

'Oh, I see.' She was very conscious of him holding her wrist in his hand. 'I'll remember.'

'Good.' On impulse, he lifted her hand to his face and bestowed a light kiss on her knuckles. 'Okay, let's go.'

Jordan's legs felt decidedly shaky as she followed him back across the road to the jeep. It was ridiculous really, she chided herself. He hadn't done anything; only brushed her knuckles with his lips, and that was nothing really. But her skin tingled where his lips had touched, and she was supremely conscious of his lean body as he swung into the jeep beside her.

He pulled up at the gates to the hotel, and Jordan was grateful, but when she went to get out his insistent words arrested her. 'When will I see you again?' he asked, and she turned to look at him with some regret.

'I—don't think——'

'How about the day after tomorrow?' he interrupted her huskily. 'I'll come and get you about—three o'clock, hmm? We can play some music. If you like my music, that is.'

'Oh, I like it.' Jordan shifted unhappily. 'I—I'd love to do that, but——'

'Three o'clock, then,' said Rhys flatly, and she took a deep breath.

'No,' she said, shaking her head. 'I—I will come, but I'll borrow Daddy's Volkswagen and drive myself.'

'Okay.' Rhys drummed his fingers against the steering wheel. 'I'll be expecting you.'

Jordan nodded, and as if unable to resist the urge to wipe the anxious expression from her face, he leant towards her and deposited a reassuring kiss on her cheek. 'Until Thursday,' he murmured, and drove away as soon as her feet touched the tarmac of the drive.

CHAPTER SIX

THE night air was a soothing balm to her aching head, and realising the harsh treatment her hair had received might be in part responsible for the painful tightness across her temples, Jordan lifted her hands and loosed the pins. Immediately the chunky braid she had secured earlier fell down over one shoulder, and almost at once she felt an easing of the tension.

It must be getting late, she thought guiltily, getting to her feet and going indoors to repair the damage. But in her bedroom, seated in front of her dressing table mirror, she regarded her refection with something like desperation. Had she changed so much? she wondered, pushing her fingers into the plait so that her hair fell silkily over her arms. This was how Rhys had liked it, she recalled, stifling the emotion the memory evoked. If she had ever fastened it up, he had always tumbled it down again, laughing and burying his face in its softness. *Rhys* . . .

Jordan went infrequently to Rhys's house in those first few weeks he was on the island. To start with, she didn't like deceiving her father, and even though she was doing nothing wrong, she still felt guilty every time she met his trusting gaze. But the time she spent with Rhys was too precious to give up, and she lived every day as it came, refusing to consider the consequences.

Rhys had rigged up one of the downstairs rooms as a studio, and except for those occasions when they went down to the beach to swim, they spent most of their time in there. Sometimes Rhys would just play her records, of other bands as well as his own, and on other visits he would play for her. He was an expert on both the guitar and the electric organ, although he told her that his organist on all his records was someone else. He also had sophisticated synthesiser equipment, and Jordan was fascinated by the sounds he could create. Only occasionally would he sing, but Jordan treasured these moments most of all. His voice, raw and untrained, had the ability to scrape every nerve in her body, and at times like these she could quite understand why the audiences at his concerts went wild with excitement. She would sit watching him, her legs drawn up, arms wrapped around her knees, feeling all her bones turning to water, and the fact that he was performing for her alone was incredibly stimulating.

Eventually, of course, her father found out what was going on. She never did discover how he had found out what she doing, though she suspected Raoul had something to do with it. Anyway, although he didn't actually forbid her to see Rhys again, Robert Lucas made his disapproval blatantly clear, and Jordan was too used to obeying her father to challenge his wishes too often.

This did not improve her relationship with Rhys. Just recently she had become aware of a certain tension between them, a strained element in his attitude towards her, which was not helped when her father banned her from using the Volkswagen to reach Planter's Point. This meant that every time they wanted to see one another, Rhys had to drive to the hotel to pick her up and take her back again afterwards. It was an unsatisfactory arrangement because their time together was so limited anyway, and after one particularly brief visit, when Jordan had

had to get home to help her father with the accounts, she was not surprised when Rhys did not arrange another assignation.

Nevertheless, it hurt, and for several days she nursed her wounded pride, telling herself it was probably for the best anyway. She was becoming too involved with him, not just physically, but emotionally, and although she was not very experienced in such relationships, she was not ignorant of the facts of life. Just *being* with Rhys had been thrilling enough in the beginning, but now she knew she wanted more from him. Every time she was with him, every time they touched—either accidentally, in the exchange of glasses of beer or lemonade, or purposely, like on the beach, when he caught her round the waist and carried her, struggling, into the waves—her blood ran like wildfire through her veins, and she wanted to wind her arms around his neck and pull his teasing mouth to hers.

Such thoughts horrified her, particularly as Rhys had given her no reason to think of him that way. He was always polite, amusing, treating her more like an engaging child than an adult, except recently, when she had suspected her company was beginning to pall. Maybe he was glad of her father's involvement to free him from an annoying obligation, she thought miserably, moping about the hotel continually until Nana Fox intervened.

Nana Fox had been Robert Lucas's nanny when he was a small boy, and although she was near retiring age, she had agreed to come and look after Karen when Jordan's mother returned to England. Jordan herself was considered too old to require a nanny, but the old coloured woman had made no distinction between them, and Jordan had shared the love she lavished so generously on the two motherless little girls.

These days, of course, Nana's role was confined to sitting on her balcony knitting, or taking ponderous walks along the beach, but both girls still visited her frequently, and there was little that went on in the hotel that she didn't know about.

It was she who noticed Jordan's preoccupation, and guessed immediately what had happened. 'Plenty of other fish in the sea,' she declared complacently, putting the finishing touches to a cardigan she had knitted for Karen. 'There's that nice Ferris boy— what's his name? Neville? Nicholas?'

'It's Neil,' said Jordan, curling up on the chair beside her. 'And I'm not interested in Neil Ferris.'

'But you are interested in Rhys Williams?' remarked the old lady dryly. 'Is that wise? I hear these pop stars build quite a reputation for themselves.'

'Rhys isn't like that.' Jordan cupped her chin on her hand and stared broodingly over the balcony rail. 'He's really nice, Nana—kind and polite, and generous. He's given me loads of tapes to play on my recorder.'

'I know, I've heard them,' responded Nana Fox with a grimace. 'All that drumming—it quite reminds me of Africa!'

Jordan giggled. 'You've never been to Africa.'

'No, but I watch television, don't I?' exclaimed her companion staunchly. Then she, too, laughed. 'So— what's your problem, Jordan? If he's so nice, why don't you go and see him? Your father hasn't forbidden you, has he? He's only expressed his disapproval.'

'He's banned me from using the Volkswagen,' muttered Jordan miserably. 'It's too far to walk to Planter's Point. Besides, I don't have the time.'

Nana Fox frowned over her sewing. 'Borrow Josef's Mini,' she remarked carelessly. 'I'm sure he'd lend it to you for an hour or so. He won't be needing it.'

'Oh, Nana, you're brilliant!' Jordan sprang off her chair and flung her arms round the old lady. 'Why didn't I think of that? Oh, thank you!'

'Just drive carefully, that's all,' declared Nana Fox severely. 'I don't want to have to face your father if you end up in the ditch.'

'I won't.' Jordan hastened towards the door. 'See you later. And thanks again.'

Josef grudgingly gave his consent for her to drive his ancient vehicle. 'You take care of her now,' he ordered, patting the bonnet affectionately. 'I don't want no bumps or scratches on this paintwork. I painted it myself.'

Jordan grinned. 'I'll be careful,' she assured him warmly, and drove away feeling free for the first time in weeks.

Weeks! She shook her head. It was two weeks since she had seen Rhys, and she pictured his surprise when she drove up in the old Mini. So long as he was at home, she amended anxiously. But where else could he be?

The Mini broke down about two hundred yards from Rhys's gate. One minute it seemed to be progressing happily, and the next it coughed and spluttered and ground to a standstill. Damn, she thought impatiently. But at least it had helped her to achieve her objective. Rhys would have to give her a tow, but that was something she would worry about later.

Managing to push the car on to the grass verge, she set off to walk the last few yards. It was very hot, and the camisole dress she had worn, because it was the prettiest thing in her wardrobe, was soon clinging to her legs. She half wished she had worn her bikini, so that she could have taken the dress off, but underneath were only her cotton briefs, which in no way resembled a bathing suit.

She heard the sound of music and voices as she turned into the drive of Rhys's house, and for a moment she faltered, uncertain of what to do next. But curiosity—and the fact that she had no means of transport back to the hotel—forced her to go on, and following the path along the side of the house, she eventually reached her goal.

The music was louder here, emanating, she suspected, from the loudspeaker system in Rhys's living room. The noise of talking and laughter had warned her of the presence of other people, but even so, Jordan was not prepared for the sight that met her startled eyes. At least half a dozen young men and women were sprawled over Rhys's verandah, with empty cans and bottles littering the flat boards at their feet. They were all in various stages of undress, from frayed denim shorts to minuscule bikinis, and one of the girls had actually shed her bikini top. Rhys himself was seated on the swinging couch, where in the past Jordan had often curled to listen to him play, plucking lazily at his guitar while two nubile females draped themselves decoratively beside him. It was like a scene from some Roman orgy, thought Jordan sickly, her imagination running away with her, and her face flamed with colour at the thought of her own naïvety.

At the same moment that Jordan saw Rhys, one of the other young men saw her, and tossing the can of beer he had been holding aside, he got unsteadily to his feet.

'Hey, don't go, pretty maiden!' he exclaimed, leaning heavily on the rail, and Jordan backed away sharply as his alcohol-laden breath engulfed her.

'*Jordan!*'

His companion's leering protest had attracted Rhys's attention, and thrusting his guitar on to the couch beside him, he too came to his feet. But Jordan was too shocked to linger. Exchanging one wounded glance with the man she had believed was beyond reproach, she turned and ran back along the path, realising as she did so she had no place else to go.

'Jordan!'

Rhys was coming after her, and although she knew it was futile, she darted into the trees at the side of his drive, stumbling over twigs and branches and scoring her bare arms with their sharp fingers. Then she was on to the beach and running, kicking off her sandals and putting as much distance between her and her pursuer as it was humanly possible to achieve.

He caught her, of course, as she had known he would. His legs were longer, and he did not have the cumbersome folds of her skirt to contend with. He could outrun her at any time, and particularly now when she was hot and breathless from the constriction of tears in her chest. Catching a handful of her hair as it billowed like a flag behind her, he slowed her progress, then deliberately tripped her up, tumbling her down on to the soft-packed sand. She tried to save herself, clutching his arm as she felt herself falling; but all she succeeded in doing was bringing him down with her, and his weight upon her body knocked all the air out of her lungs.

She lay there panting, her hair a glory of sun-streaked silk about her, her breasts clearly outlined beneath the thin cotton of her dress as she struggled to regain her breath, her eyes brimming with unshed tears—and Rhys lost his head. With a groan of submission he covered her mouth with his own, and all the hot tearful accusations Jordan had been going to fling at him were stifled by the hungry pressure of his lips.

His mouth was firm and persuasive, easily disposing of her immature reluctance, and parting her lips with sensual insistence. Her senses swam as he plundered the moist sweetness she gave up to him, and the intimate caress of his mouth evoked sensations she had never dreamed existed. With a little moan, she wound her arms around his neck and arched her body towards him, responding instinctively to the needs he was creating. She didn't care about where she was, or that anyone might see them. She wanted to prolong the moment, and the exquisite pleasure of his touch.

'Oh, Jordan!' he muttered at last, easing his weight from her so that he could look down at her, and Jordan's colour deepened beneath his intense appraisal. What must he be thinking? she wondered, ashamed of the way she had reacted, and her arms fell to her sides as she recalled what she had interrupted back at the house.

'I'm sorry,' she said unsteadily, putting up a hand to her hair, and with a groan he took her hand in his and raised it to his lips. This time he pressed his face to her palm, and the sensuous tip of his tongue was wet against her skin.

'Don't be sorry,' he said huskily. 'I've been wanting to do this for weeks. Only I didn't know how you'd react, and I didn't want to drive you away.'

'Is that why you've brought in reinforcements?' she asked bitterly, withdrawing her hand from his grasp and turning her face away, and Rhys uttered an oath as he forced her to look at him.

'They're not reinforcements,' he told her harshly. 'If you're referring to the girls, they're not my concern. Chas brought them here—Charlie Pepper, for your information. He's the drummer with the band, and the rest of them either play for me, or hang around with those who do. Does that satisfy you?'

Jordan lifted one shoulder. 'It's nothing to do with me.'

'No, it's not,' Rhys agreed briefly, 'but you're making it so. Why the hell did you charge off like that? What did you think you'd seen, for God's sake?'

'I saw *you*,' said Jordan shakily, and Rhys's eyes darkened.

'And that bothered you?' he demanded, one hand moving almost absently to her shoulder, brushing the tendrils of hair aside and flicking the strap of her camisole over her arm.

'I—yes,' she admitted unwillingly, unable to lie to him when his eyes were so intent upon hers, and he expelled his breath on a shuddering sigh.

'Good!'

'Good?'

'Yes, good,' he said, his fingers still stroking the exposed skin of her shoulder. 'But you have nothing to worry about.'

'I wasn't worried,' exclaimed Jordan hotly, angry suddenly at his apparent arrogance. 'You'd better let me get up. Your—friends—will be wondering what you're doing.'

'They know better than to come and find out,' responded Rhys, moving so that he was lying between her trembling legs. 'You're beautiful, and I'm crazy about you. Does that make you feel better?'

Jordan moved her head unsteadily from side to side, but his tongue brushing the palpitating mound of her breasts, visible above the low-cut rim of her bodice was an intoxicating inducement. The moist caress was like an abrasion to skin already sensitised by his nearness, and Jordan's legs went weak as he continued his exploration.

The other strap was disposed of and Rhys pushed the elasticated bodice of the dress down so that her breasts emerged, aroused and swollen. 'You mustn't,' Jordan whispered, making a token move to protect

herself, but Rhys's mouth deterred her, and his
muffled: 'Why not?' against one engorged peak
seemed to negate her objections. He moved slowly,
but sensually, arousing feelings she had not known she
possessed, and she was soon breathless and clinging to
him.

Her fingers curled around his nape, digging into the
silky smooth hair she found there, and glorying in his
apparent vulnerability. Her hands were free to roam
over his body—naked, save for the shabby denim
shorts he invariably wore around the house—and he
groaned when she found some sensitive spot and
exploited it. Then he possessed her mouth again until
she was drugged and incoherent.

His own response was evident. Jordan had never felt
the rigid thrust of a man's desire before, but there was
something dangerously exciting in knowing she could
arouse him like this. The thin barrier of his shorts and
her skirt and panties was little protection from the
pulsating muscle that swelled against her stomach, and
she found herself moving to accommodate him.

'Oh, *God*!' His shuddering withdrawal was unwelcome, and Jordan refused to let him go, her arms
around his neck soft and clinging. 'Come on,' he
groaned, extricating himself with difficulty. 'Jordan,
this has got to stop——'

'Why?'

'Why?' he muttered harshly. 'Because you don't
know what you're doing, and sure as hell, I don't.'

'Why not?' Jordan looked up at him anxiously, her
hands still lingering on his shoulders. 'Didn't you
want to kiss me?'

'Oh, Jordan!' Rhys pressed his hands down on the
sand at either side of her and pushed himself back on
to his knees. 'You know better than that.'

'Then why——'

She levered herself up on her elbows, but becoming aware of her state of undress, she hastily pulled the bodice of her dress back into place, and Rhys closed his eyes for a moment against the unconscious sexuality of her movements.

'That's why,' he said, jack-knifing to his feet and looking down at her. 'You may be seventeen, Jordan, and back home a girl of that age would consider she knew the score. But you're not like the girls back home, and I——' he broke off to push the thick hair back from his forehead—'oh, God! I don't want to spoil what we have.'

'How could we spoil this?' Jordan blinked in some confusion, and then, holding out her hand, she invited him to pull her to her feet. But when he had done so, she fell against him, and his arms went automatically round her to support her.

Immediately her face turned up to his, and unable to resist the open invitation of her mouth, he bent his head to hers. 'I love you,' she breathed against his lips, and her husky words caused him to gather her even closer.

'You're crazy,' he muttered, but he didn't push her away, and the kiss deepened and lengthened to a passionate obeisance.

They walked back to the house together, their arms around each other, and Chas Pepper and the other members of the party regarded them with good-humoured tolerance.

'I should have known you'd have everything under control here, Williams,' the drummer declared in grudging deference. 'Who is she? When did you find her?'

'I bought this house from her father,' retorted Rhys easily, unperturbed by their frank inquisitiveness. He looked down into Jordan's face and she saw the possessive light smouldering in his eyes. 'So hands off—she's mine. Aren't you?'

Jordan coloured. 'Do you want me to tell you—or them?' she murmured, refusing to let him disconcert her, and his arm about her shoulders enfolded her against him.

'They'll be leaving soon,' he averred, casting a meaningful glance in Chas's direction, and the drummer grimaced disappointedly as he shifted from his position on the verandah rail.

'What a party this has turned out to be,' he muttered, finishing the beer in his can. 'Get your clothes on, Susie. We've got our marching orders.'

'Oh, but——' Jordan looked troubled now. 'Please—don't send them away because of me, Rhys. I—er—I have to get back to the hotel soon.'

Rhys's face hardened slightly. 'Your father?'

'Partly.' She paused. 'But I borrowed Josef's Mini to get here and it broke down, just up the road from the house.'

'Oh, great!' Rhys released her to counter Chas's undisguised delight at this turn of events. 'Okay, you lot: Dave, Luke, you know something about engines, don't you? Come on, we'll go and check the damage.'

While the four men went to find the Mini, Jordan found herself at the mercy of the other girls present. There were three of them: two blondes and a redhead, the latter being the one Chas had called Susie, and who was presently retying the bra of her bikini.

'How long have you known, Rhys?' one of the blondes asked, her brows arching insolently. 'I thought I knew all his girl-friends.'

'Well, evidently you don't,' retorted Susie, giving Jordan time to weather this particular piece of information. 'Take no notice of Petra, kid. She's only jealous.'

'I am not.' Petra reached for a wrap-around mini-skirt, and fastened it about her hips. 'Rhys always was kind to children. Why should he change now?'

'Miaow,' mocked Susie, getting to her feet. 'What's your name, kid? We know it's Lucas, but what else?'

'Jordan,' said Jordan uncomfortably, unused to the cut and thrust of female bitchery. 'And I've known Rhys for about six weeks. Ever since he came to the island.'

'You're kind of young for him, aren't you?' queried the girl who had not previously entered the conversation, and Jordan's face flamed. The other girl's words had not been said spitefully, but both Petra and Susie were waiting for her answer, and it was difficult to think of a clever response.

'I don't think so,' she said at last, lifting her shoulders, and Susie came to the rescue again.

'Nor do I,' she declared, tossing back her mane of bright red hair. Her eyes challenged the other girls. 'Remember Jennifer.'

'Jennifer wasn't a kid!' exclaimed Petra impatiently, but Susie was not deterred.

'I know,' she said meaningfully, her expression telling her companions something it could not tell Jordan, and the blonde who had spoken last nodded.

'I get your point,' she remarked, bending to take some cigarettes out of a flowered beach bag. 'Okay. So what are we doing?'

'That's what I'd like to know,' said Petra, giving Jordan a contemptuous glance. 'Rhys said nothing about her when he invited us here.'

'That's his business,' said Susie wryly.

'But how long is it likely to last?' exclaimed Petra impatiently, only to turn away in frustration when

Rhys himself vaulted up on to the verandah beside her.

'A lifetime, I hope,' he answered, putting a possessive arm about Jordan's waist. He drew her back against him so that she could feel his instantaneous response. 'Thanks for entertaining Jordan, Petra. I knew I could rely on you.'

Petra said nothing, and Jordan could hardly think with his bronzed arm brushing her breasts and the heat of his body against her buttocks. But she had to say something, and taking a deep breath she asked: 'Did you find the car?'

'We did.' Rhys sounded amused now. 'And it's fixed. Or at least it will be, in a couple of minutes.' He rubbed his cheek against her hair, causing Petra's lips to tighten in irritation. 'Don't you know you should always check the petrol gauge?'

Maybe she should have paid more attention to what Petra had said, thought Jordan, getting up from her dressing table. Every word all three girls had spoken had been relevant, only she had been too bemused to see it at the time. They had even indirectly warned her about Jennifer, if she had had the sense to listen.

She sighed. If only things could have been different! They had been happy together, albeit that happiness was founded on a false premise, but she had loved him. She had never dreamed that anything could come between them, and although that seemed a naïve assumption now, at the time it had not seemed so foolish. He had said he was in love with her; he had even talked about marriage; and she had defied her father's warnings to take what Rhys had offered.

Shaking her head, she moved towards the door. Her

headache had eased considerably, but she knew if she allowed this regression into the past to continue it could well return. Nevertheless, she did wish she had handled tonight's interview with more maturity. The last thing she wanted was for him to think she was still carrying a torch for him.

CHAPTER SEVEN

'DADDY!'

Lucy's voice floated up from the terrace below, and Rhys knew he couldn't ignore it. Right now, he could do without his daughter's company, but as he had no intention of explaining why, he could hardly tell her that.

He was in a foul mood. He had been in a foul mood since the confrontation with Jordan the night before, and the amount of alcohol he had consumed before he eventually crawled into bed had left his system hungover and his mouth tasting like a sewer. He felt dour and unsociable, and it took an effort to push himself up from the lounging chair on the balcony and walk to the rail.

'I'm here,' he answered now, resting his hands on the wrought iron as he looked down at her. In her skimpy blue and white bikini, her skin darkening daily to a deeper tan, Lucy looked the picture of health, but her expression was petulant as she met his jaded gaze. 'What do you want?' he asked, trying to be tolerant. 'I've got a headache.' *Which was true.* 'If you need something, ask Rosa or Tomas. I'm working.' *Which wasn't!*

Lucy's lower lip jutted. 'I can't ask the Simms,' she retorted sulkily. 'You said you'd go swimming with me this morning. I've been waiting for ages, and you're not even dressed!'

'Oh, that!' Rhys pushed his hand into the unruly tangle of his hair, looking down guiltily at his legs, bare beneath the silk hem of his robe. 'I forgot.'

'You seem to be forgetting a lot of things lately,' said Lucy accusingly. 'Like making that reservation for dinner yesterday evening. I was looking forward to some hotel food for a change. Instead of which, we had to make do with Rosa's gumbo!'

'I shouldn't let her hear you speaking so disparagingly of it,' remarked Rhys dryly, flexing his shoulder muscles. 'Oh, all right. I'll be down in a few minutes. Just give me time to put on my shorts and comb my hair.'

'Okay.'

Lucy was placated, and Rhys turned away from the rail to enter the bedroom behind the balcony. The room he was occupying was decorated in shades of cream and beige, and he welcomed its restful coolness. Light walls, lit by locally-painted watercolours, framed the darkwood furniture, most of which had been locally made, too. The bed was four-postered and old-fashioned in design, but a modern interior-sprung mattress bought in Nassau made it superbly comfortable, and the pattern of the fine linen sheets and pillowcases was echoed in the raw silk curtains at the windows.

It was a comfortable room, though by no means as luxurious as the one next door. Ten years ago, his desire to enjoy the accoutrements of success had led him to install a quadraphonic stereo system in both his bedroom and his bathroom, and the circular sunken bath with its smoked glass surround and gold taps was a further indication of his search for identity. These days, however, such sybaritic tendencies had left him, and besides, he had no wish now to sleep in the bed he and Jordan had once shared.

Shedding his robe now, he walked naked into the bathroom adjoining the bedroom and examined his reflection in the mirror above the handbasin without satisfaction. There were pouches beneath his eyes that had not been there when he left Nassau ten days ago, he acknowledged impatiently, so why did he stay? It wasn't as if he would be depriving Lucy of a holiday. They could stay in Nassau, at the Beach Hotel, and enjoy themselves just as much, with the added attraction of shops and entertainment on their doorstep.

Shaking his head, he bent to sluice his face with water, then used the electric toothbrush before lifting a cream towel from the metal rack above the clothes basket. Burying his face in its soft folds, he wondered why he didn't just pack up and go. His wisest course would be to put this house up for sale. Ten years on, he should make a handsome profit, and he could use the extra money to buy a home in California or Hawaii, or some other place that took his fancy.

Sighing, he tossed the towel aside and resumed his self-contemplation. He needed a shave, he thought, running his hand experimentally along his jawline. But that could wait, he decided, noticing the slight tremor in his fingers. The way he felt right now, he might easily cut his throat, and he had no wish to put temptation in his way.

Swearing savagely, he turned and walked back into the bedroom. He had been a fool to come here, and he was an even bigger fool for staying. After last night's little fiasco, he had no illusions that Jordan might have forgiven him. Although she had tried to be civil, it had obviously been an effort, and it hadn't taken much to tear aside the façade of polite indifference she had affected. She hated him; she hated both of them; and by staying here he was running the risk of Lucy finding out why.

As he pulled on the black shorts he wore to swim in, his face contorted angrily. What was the matter with him? he asked himself harshly. What did he care what

Jordan Lucas thought of him? She was part of the past, not the present, and that was why he was staying. Because if he walked out now, he would never be able to convince himself he had not been running away.

Down on the beach, a little of his depression left him. Who could remain unmoved in such surroundings? he thought impatiently. White sand, blue-green water, waving palms—it was an island paradise, and he would not have been human if he hadn't found some enjoyment in it.

Lucy was waiting for him, and summoning all his reserves of energy, Rhys uttered a cry and caught her around her waist. Hustling her, squealing and struggling, into the water, however, he was irresistibly reminded of other occasions when Jordan had responded in much the same way. He didn't want to think of such things, but it was impossible not to compare his daughter's reactions with Jordan's playful responses, and once they were both engulfed by the waves, he swam strongly away. Jordan had loved the water, still did probably, and because she was a native of the island and not just a holidaymaker, her skin had been deeply tanned. Except where her bikini covered, Rhys remembered now, feeling an unwelcome heat in his loins. Her breasts and the rounded softness of her rear had been so much paler, until he had persuaded her to sunbathe without any clothes at all . . .

'Daddy!' Once again, Lucy's voice broke into his mood, and he looked half impatiently towards the shallows where she was still splashing about. 'Who's that?' Lucy added, pointing to a slim figure standing motionless on their verandah, and Rhys felt an unfamiliar constriction in his gut. He would have recognised Jordan anywhere, let alone on his verandah, where he had seen her so many times before.

'I—it's Miss Lucas,' he answered now, swimming

back to shallow water and wading up on to the beach.
'You remember? You met her last night.' *And what the
hell is she doing here?* he added silently.

'Oh, yes.' Lucy waded out beside him, looking
resentfully towards the house. 'Well, what does she
want? I paid for my drink with that money you gave
me.'

Rhys shook his head and swept back his wet hair
with a careless hand. 'How should I know?' he
countered sharply, too disturbed to moderate his tone.
And then, as she started to accompany him up the
beach, he appended: 'You stay here. I'll be back in a
few minutes.'

'But, Daddy——'

'A few minutes,' Rhys repeated flatly, and leaving
her sulking, he strode up the beach.

Jordan stepped back as he came up the steps of the
verandah, and he saw at once how nervous she was.
But at least she hadn't scraped her hair back from her
face this morning, he reflected, even if the matronly
chignon was no more to his taste. She looked pale and
tired, the outfit of beige shirt and matching cotton
pants hardly complimenting her tan, and he thought at
once how thin she looked, and then again, how
young . . .

'Hello, Rhys,' she murmured, putting her hands
behind her back in an unconsciously childish gesture.
'I—er—Rosa told me where you were, and although I
know you said you didn't want me to come here, I felt
I had to apologise.'

'Apologise?' Rhys felt blank and was sure he looked
it. 'Apologise for what?'

'For last night,' said Jordan at once, shifting from
one foot to the other. 'I behaved—stupidly; senselessly.
I don't know what you must have thought of me.' She
paused, then added stiffly: 'I'd just like to say that I'm

sorry, and that naturally you're welcome to dine at the hotel any time you like.'

Rhys sought the towel he had left lying on a chair on his way down to the beach, and rubbed absently at his chest and arms. Then he looped it round his neck and towelled his hair as he strove to absorb this new development. Though the temptation was there, he didn't altogether believe her explanation, and he couldn't help wondering what private notion had caused her to abandon her hostility. Last night he would have sworn that nothing could change her mind, yet here she was, apparently repentant and asking his pardon.

While he was still assimiliating what she had said, Jordan shifted sideways towards the steps that gave access to the path that circled the house. Watching her, Rhys was almost convinced she was relieved by his failure to answer, and the thought crossed his mind that she had wanted to disconcert him.

'I'd better go,' she said. 'I'm interrupting your swim, and I'm sure your daughter won't thank me for it. Thanks for listening to me. I hope I've convinced you now that—that there are no hard feelings——'

'Just a minute.' Rhys's motive powers started to function again, and before she could start down the steps, his fingers curled round her arm. Her skin felt strange, almost familiar, and he knew a fleeting desire to release her before that familiarity took a hold of him. But he quelled the treacherous impulse and deliberately tightened his grip. 'Why don't you stay and have some coffee? I'm sure Rosa would be happy to oblige. She's missed you.'

His eyes held hers determinedly, and he saw the flickering panic that came and went in her taut gaze. She *was* afraid of him, he thought incredulously. But why? For God's sake, what did she expect him to do with Lucy looking on?

'I—I really should be getting back,' she faltered, and her uneasy movement made him intensely aware of her fragility. Her arm felt so insubstantial in his grasp, the bone tenuous and brittle, easy to snap.

'Not yet,' he asserted harshly, giving in to a totally selfish desire to make her squirm. 'After all, it isn't every day that old—friends get together. And I'd like to hear what you've been doing since I went away.'

For a moment he thought she was going to defy him. An angry little flame had taken the place of the panic in her grey eyes, and Rhys was reminded of how easy it had been to upset her the night before. He didn't want that to happen now, not until he had had time to gauge her real reasons for coming here, and the tight smile he summoned was a deliberate attempt to defuse the situation.

'I—I—oh, all right,' she capitulated unwillingly, and he withdrew his fingers from her arm with some reluctance.

'Good.' He gestured towards one of the comfortable loungers. 'Won't you sit down?'

She sat, albeit on the edge of her seat, and after a momentary hesitation, Rhys excused himself to go and speak to Rosalie. He would like to have changed, too. His shorts were sticking to him, but he was afraid if he disappeared for too long Jordan might not be here when he got back, so he confined his absence to speaking to the housekeeper.

'Could we have some coffee, Rosa?' he requested, supporting himself against the frame of the kitchen door, and she looked up at him quizzically.

'Who for? You and Lucy?' she enquired innocently, and his mouth drew down at the implied criticism.

'For Lucy and me, yes,' he conceded, inclining his head. 'But add a third cup, will you?'

'For Missy Jordan?' suggested Rosalie, abandoning

the vegetables she had been preparing and drying her hands on her apron, and Rhys sighed.

'As you know,' he agreed flatly. 'Any objections?'

'Me?' Rosalie's dark eyes widened, and Rhys's patience shredded.

'Just bring the coffee, will you?' he ordered, and swinging on his heel he made his way back to the verandah.

Jordan was still sitting where he had left her, and pausing for a moment in the shadows of the living room, Rhys watched her unobserved. She had changed, he thought grimly; who hadn't? But it was more than just a thinning of her features, and the fact that the lush vitality of youth had given way to a fine-boned beauty. The change was more fundamental than that. She seemed to have lost the ability to relax, with him at least, and although he despised the impulse, he knew an overwhelming urge to regain her confidence.

As if sensing his regard, she turned suddenly, and he came swiftly out of the shadows to join her. 'Coffee's on the way,' he remarked, propping his hips against the wooden handrail. 'Rosa's pleased to see you. She told me how you'd looked after the house while I was away. I should have thanked you.'

'It's not necessary.' Jordan shifted a little way back on her seat, rubbing the palms of her hands over the knees of her pants as she did so. 'I—oh, here's your daughter.' Her eyes wavered. 'She's a lot like you, isn't she?'

Rhys's mouth compressed. 'Do you think so?' he responded, turning with some impatience as Lucy mounted the steps beside him. 'I guess you got tired of waiting,' he added, controlling his temper with difficulty. 'You know Miss Lucas, don't you?'

Lucy nodded, flicking a careless glance in Jordan's direction. 'You said you wouldn't be long, Daddy,' she exclaimed, flouncing into the chair beside their guest. 'What does Miss Lucas want? Did you explain about the drinks?'

Rhys gave her a warning look. 'Miss Lucas is just visiting, Lucy,' he declared. 'Like I told you last night, she and I are old friends. We knew one another—quite well, when I lived here ten years ago.'

'Was that before Mummy and I came here?' asked Lucy idly, and Rhys wondered if she suspected that their relationship had been more than he had said.

'Yes, before that,' Jordan answered her tautly, before he could speak. 'I never knew your mother. I wish I had.'

Lucy looked smug, and for the first time in his life Rhys wanted to slap her. Why the hell couldn't she have left them alone? he thought savagely. He would achieve nothing with his daughter looking on, adding her own kind of fuel to the conversation. But what did he hope to achieve anyway? he asked himself fiercely. He had sworn never to speak to Jordan again, and yet here he was, offering her coffee and wanting to defend her against his daughter.

Rosalie's arrival with the coffee put paid to his inner flagellation, and after the woman had set the tray on the glass-topped table, she turned warmly to Jordan. 'You see,' she said, 'he ain' so bad. Just a man, that's all. Just a man.'

Jordan flushed, and Lucy's brows drew together as she surveyed the other girl's embarrassment. With a feeling of impotence, Rhys heard Jordan make some discomfited retort, and then, moving swiftly, he squatted down beside the tray. Clattering cups into saucers, he made Rosalie's further presence unnecessary, and with a significant shrug of her shoulders the housekeeper left them.

'I'll do that, Daddy,' protested Lucy, stretching out her hand, but Rhys merely shook his head.

'Cream and sugar?' he enquired of Jordan, and moistening her lips with an unknowingly provocative tongue, she made an involuntary gesture.

'Just cream, please,' she said, avoiding his eyes, and Rhys poured the coffee and handed it to her.

He noticed she took care not to touch his fingers as she lifted the generous American-style cup out of his hand, and his lips tightened as he attended to Lucy's needs and his own. In all honesty, he was glad of the reviving taste of the beverage, which he took black and sweet, the hangover he had experienced earlier returning in these moments of tension. Why the hell hadn't he let her go when she wanted to? he flayed himself impatiently, and then quelled his rising frustration by turning to stare out across the white coral sand to the ocean beyond.

'You're not married, Miss Lucas,' Lucy remarked suddenly, and although the comment was innocent enough, Rhys's attention was dragged back to the present.

'No,' Jordan was responding now. 'Not yet,' she added, and the faint smile that lifted her lips was irritatingly reminiscent.

'Not yet?' echoed Lucy, with interest. 'Does that mean you may be getting married in the near future?'

No! he wanted to answer her. It didn't mean anything of the kind, but Jordan had her own reply ready.

'Possibly,' she answered now, setting her cup down on the tray, and he wondered if she heard his sudden intake of breath. 'Neil, that's my—boy-friend, he doesn't want to wait much longer.'

'I see.' Lucy flicked a glance up at her father. 'Do you know Miss Lucas's boy-friend, Daddy?'

Rhys felt as if his features were frozen. *Neil!* he was berating himself fiercely. *Neil who?*

'I don't know,' he managed now, answering his daughter's question. His tawny eyes rested on Jordan with unknowing cruelty. 'Miss Lucas no doubt has a lot of friends.'

'It's Neil Ferris, actually,' said Jordan tautly. 'I don't believe you met him.'

'I don't believe I did,' he essayed, finishing his own coffee and moving forward to pour himself a second cup. 'I assume Mr Ferris lives on the island.'

'Yes.' Jordan paused. 'He owns the other hotel, Coral Cay.'

'How convenient!' Rhys's sarcasm was unmistakable. 'By getting married, you'll corner the market, won't you?'

'That's hardly a good enough reason for getting married,' retorted Jordan defensively, but Rhys had little sympathy for her now.

'What would you say constituted a quotes good enough reason close quotes?' he asked harshly, and Jordan stiffened.

'Having children, perhaps?' she countered swiftly, and his mouth compressed.

'Oh, yes.' He set his empty cup down on the tray with a definite click. 'I'd forgotten that one.'

'Had you?' Jordan's eyes flashed, and the sudden animation of her features was fascinating. But he had no time to enjoy it. 'I suppose it's easy to forget something like that when you have so much else to think about.'

Rhys's mouth snapped shut over the angry retort he had been about to make. If he wasn't careful they'd end up rowing as they had done the night before, and he had no wish for Lucy to witness such a surrendering of his self-control.

Forcing a tight smile to his lips, he bowed his head in silent acknowledgement of her victory, and now

Jordan had the grace to look discomfited. Getting to her feet, she pushed her hands into the pockets of her slacks and faced him.

'I think I'd better be going,' she said stiffly. 'Thank you for the coffee. It was delicious.'

'My pleasure.' Rhys straightened. 'I'll walk you to the gate.'

'That's not necessary——'

'Nevertheless, I will,' he averred, stepping aside so that she could precede him down the steps. 'After you.'

He was aware that Lucy's eyes followed them as they took the path that led round to the drive, and then the wall of the house and the luxuriant bank of foliage hid them from her sight. The buggy was waiting at the gate, but before she could swing herself into the seat and escape him, he stopped her.

'That was pretty despicable, wasn't it?' he demanded, and he could tell she knew exactly what he meant.

'What you did was pretty despicable!' she retorted unevenly. 'I'm sorry if I've made things difficult for you, but you shouldn't have baited me like that.'

'Baited you?' Rhys's temper flared. 'What would you call what you did? Regaling Lucy with all that stuff about Neil Ferris! Who the hell is Neil Ferris? I'd like to meet him. If he meets your fastidious requirements, he must be a real pain!'

Jordan's palm stung like mad against his cheek, and abandoning any attempt to reason with her, Rhys looped an arm around her neck and jerked her towards him. 'Bitch,' he snarled, bending his head and grinding his mouth into hers until he tasted her blood on his tongue. There was no gentleness in his kiss, only the desire to hurt and gorge himself with that satisfaction. 'I could kill you,' he muttered, when he released her mouth to bury his face in the quivering flesh at her nape, and Jordan could be left in no doubt that he meant what he said.

The futile objections she had offered had been stifled by his superior strength, and when he released her now, she sagged against the bonnet of the buggy, wiping a smear of red from her lips. 'Don't—don't you ever touch me again!' she choked, her face twisting in sick disgust. 'You're—you're an animal!'

'As you made me,' retorted Rhys, refusing to feel any shame for what he had done. 'And you weren't always so particular!'

Jordan shook her head blindly, as if to negate his accusation, and groping her way along the vehicle, she scrambled in behind the wheel. He doubted she was in a fit state to drive, but pride—and an aversion to prolong the situation—made him turn away, and he heard the engine fire and the tyres squeal as he walked back up the drive.

Lucy was still lounging on the verandah, but her face was red, as if she had suffered some exertion, and although he suspected it, he was too weary to ask if she had been eavesdropping. What the hell! She was bound to find out sooner or later that he and Jordan had once been close, he thought dispiritedly. He was surprised Rosa hadn't dropped a hint already, but didn't particularly care. Not now. So long as that was all she learned, he reflected, as he flung himself into a chair.

CHAPTER EIGHT

RHYS had not intended to get involved with Jordan Lucas.

He had bought the house on Eleutha because he had wanted somewhere of his own, where he could escape from the pressures his public life was putting upon him. The idea of having a home in such an idyllic spot had appealed to the artistic side of his nature, and in a more practical sense the house at Planter's Point could provide him with a place to work far away from commercial influences.

His plans for building a sound studio on the island had never been realised, primarily because of his involvement with Jordan. And after the affair was all over, he had decided it had been an impractical suggestion at best. But that had been while he was still feeling raw in the aftermath of their break-up, and the prospect of returning to Eleutha for any purpose had seemed totally unacceptable. Now, however, with the objectivity of distance, he could regret that emotive decision, even if the reasons for its making were still as relevant as ever.

But, ten years ago, his arrival on the island had given him no forewarning of what was to come. The house was beautiful—but he had known that in advance. The agent he had hired to handle the sale for him had assured him of its suitability, and he had provided dozens of photographs for Rhys to study in the evenings after another of his exhausting schedule of concerts. Rhys had instantly felt able to relax there, and if his meeting with Robert Lucas had not been entirely harmonious, the island was big enough for them to avoid one another quite satisfactorily.

However, Rhys had not bargained for his own immediate, and quite insensible, attraction for Robert Lucas's elder daughter. From the first moment he saw her, flushed and grubby, and evidently hot with embarrassment, he had felt an unfamiliar desire to protect her, and when his housekeeper had walked out on him he had jumped at the excuse to see Jordan again.

Of course, she was too young. He had told himself that a hundred times. And it would be madness to get involved with one of the local girls, when he had bought a house here and intended to stay. He knew that, too. But circumstances, and his own recklessness, had served to undermine his determination, and when he saw her again, slim and golden in her skimpy shorts, he had not been able to resist temptation.

Even so, he had succeeded in controlling their relationship for the first few weeks. They spent a lot of time together, it was true, but apart from in play, he had not laid a hand on her. It had not been easy, and there had been times, he knew, when the situation between them became somewhat strained, due to the unwelcome awareness of his own sexuality. But he might have restrained his baser impulses if Jordan herself had not precipitated their release.

Once Robert Lucas had found out about his daughter's association with the undesirable alien and forbidden her the use of his car, Rhys had realised it could give him the opportunity to withdraw from their relationship before anything irreparable happened. Without transport Jordan could not come to the house, and so long as he stayed away from her, he could handle his own feelings. He even invited the rest of the band to join him, knowing he could rely on Chas Pepper to bring some girls along to distract him.

It hadn't worked. He had been moody and irritable all the time they were there, and Jordan's unexpected arrival overturned all his carefully devised plans. As soon as he saw her, he knew it was no good. He wanted her—*God*! how he wanted her—and if he hadn't come to his senses, he'd have taken her there, on the beach, in view of anyone who cared to watch . . .

Rhys groaned now, folding his arms beneath his head as he lay supine on the sand. The sun was approaching its noonday zenith, and he could tell from the way Lucy was splashing about in the shallows that she was getting bored with her own company. He hadn't been very sociable since Jordan's departure, and he suspected his daughter was thinking about the other girl, too.

If only he could forget, he thought savagely, thrusting himself into a sitting position and looping one arm protectively over his head. But the memories just kept on coming—not least, the first time they made love . . .

It was almost two weeks before Jordan had come to the house again, two weeks during which time Rhys was able to do nothing—not eat, not sleep, not work; he simply spent his time roaming from room to room, or pacing the empty spaces of the beach, caring little for his health, or his appearance, or his surroundings.

At first he suspected her father had forbidden her to visit him again. Had Robert Lucas observed his daughter's return in Josef's Mini and been angry at this obvious means of thwarting him, Rhys wondered. But although he telephoned the hotel several times and left messages for her to call him, he had no response, and he was eventually forced to assume that he had frightened her off.

He did think of driving to the hotel and forcing a confrontation, but the prospect of running into her father was not one he cared to face. If Jordan chose not to see him again, that was her decision. If her father was trying to force his will upon her, Rhys knew he could not depend on his own temper staying in check. In his present volatile state, he could quite easily resort to violence, and he didn't think Jordan would appreciate his uncontrolled intervention.

Then one afternoon, when the sun was trapped behind a bank of overhanging cloud and Rhys was trapped in his studio, trying to make some headway with the melody he was composing, Jordan appeared. She had evidently used some exertion to get here, because her face was flushed and moist with heat, and her shirt and shorts were sticking to her. When he came in answer to her uncertain call, she swayed a little unsteadily, and he took a swift look at her tremulous face before bidding her to take a seat.

'I'll get some iced juice,' he said tautly, gesturing towards one of the cushioned loungers. 'Sit down before you fall down. You can tell me about it when I come back.'

Rosalie was snoozing in her chair on the back step, and Rhys helped himself to the jug of iced orange juice in the fridge, collecting some glasses on his way back to the verandah. When he emerged from the house, he found Jordan stretched out on the striped recliner, but she opened her eyes at his approach and struggled into a sitting position.

'Here,' he said, squatting down on his haunches beside her, and filling a glass with the cool sweet liquid. 'You must be dehydrated,' he added, as she gulped at it greedily. 'What the hell have you been doing? Running?

'Cy-cycling, actually,' said Jordan at last, wiping a

smear of orange juice from her chin with the back of her hand. 'I cycled here.' She sighed. 'I—I didn't realise it was so far!'

Rhys gazed at her in disbelief. 'You've bicycled all the way from the hotel!'

'Yes,' Jordan nodded, the ponytail securing her long hair bobbing as she did so. 'There was no other way,' she appended simply, a little of the hectic colour receding from her cheeks. 'I wanted to see you.'

'Jordan!' His voice was knowingly harsh as he said her name, and pushing himself to his feet he stood looking down at her. 'You must be crazy, in this heat,' he muttered, surveying her without compassion. 'I suggest you go and take a shower and rest for a while. I wouldn't like your father to think I was responsible for the way you look now.'

Her face lost much of its animation at his deliberately scathing words, and she looked down at her sunburned arms and legs, evidently chastened by his apparent contempt.

'I don't care what my father thinks,' she declared after a moment, then got determinedly to her feet. 'I—I will take that shower, if you don't mind. I—I do feel rather—sticky.'

It was all Rhys could do to prevent himself from taking her in his arms there and then, but although her burst of defiance had intrigued him, experience had made him wary. 'Okay,' he said, gesturing indoors. 'I guess you know where everything is. If you need anything else, just give me a shout.'

'Thanks.'

Jordan moved past him, and Rhys stepped back against the verandah rail. He wondered what she was thinking, what thoughts had caused that sudden furrowing of her brow as she stepped into the house, then he turned his back on the pathetic picture she made as she limped painfully across his living room. Why had she really come here? he wondered. Could he really believe she wanted to see him when she had waited so long without contacting him? Or was it simply a case of defying her father, in whatever fashion she knew would annoy him most?

In spite of his suspicions, Rhys was unable to remain inactive with Jordan upstairs, using his bathroom, standing naked under his shower. Leaving the verandah, he walked impatiently into his studio, and ignoring the erratic pulsing of his heart, he determinedly picked up his guitar. But his fingers felt thick and clumsy, discordant on the strings, and he was thrusting it aside irritably when he heard Jordan's troubled call.

Striding out into the hall, he reached the foot of the stairs and looked up. 'Yes?' he answered tautly. 'Is something wrong?'

Jordan appeared, looking over the rail of the balcony above him, and his stomach muscles tightened at the sight of her wrapped in his towelling bathrobe. 'I—do you have any shampoo?' she ventured, holding the lapels closely together. 'I've had a shower, but I got my hair wet, and I couldn't find anything to wash it with.'

Rhys expelled his breath heavily, and then mounted the stairs two at a time. 'It's in the cabinet above the handbasin,' he said, passing her without looking at her, entering his bedroom and walking through it to the bathroom beyond. 'There.' He extracted a plastic container filled with an expensive preparation bought for him by an ardent admirer. 'That should do. I'm unlikely to use it.'

'Oh? Why?'

Jordan looked at him with wide enquiring eyes, and if he hadn't known better, Rhys would have half believed she was deliberately drawing his attention to her. As it was, he had to steel himself to look into those smoky grey eyes, to hold himself rigid and not allow his gaze to wander over the yielding curves of her body, sensuously concealed by the wraparound folds of his robe.

'It's too—perfumed for my taste,' he answered swiftly, glancing into the shower cubicle behind her. 'I see you managed to sort out the taps,' he added, keeping the conversation impersonal. 'The water's never completely cold, as you probably know, but it's refreshing.'

'It's a beautiful bathroom,' said Jordan admiringly. 'Gold taps, and smoked mirrors! Very sexy!'

'How would you know?'

The words were out before he could prevent them, and Jordan wrapped the bathrobe even closer about her. 'I—I wouldn't, of course,' she murmured, making him feel even worse. Then, tilting her head, she looked up at him, and he felt the unwanted heat invading his loins. 'Tell me, Rhys—are you angry with me?'

Rhys clenched his fists. 'Angry with you?' he said tautly, hearing the bitter note in his voice and despising himself for it. 'Why should I be angry with you?' He paused, then went on harshly: 'Apart from waiting for you to come—apart from phoning you and expecting you to at least acknowledge my calls—apart from not being able to eat, or sleep, or work! Why should I be angry with you?'

Jordan sighed. 'I wanted to come——'

'Did you?' The scepticism was evident.

'Yes.' She caught her lower lip between her teeth and shifted from one bare foot to the other. 'But I couldn't.'

'Because of your father?'

He was scathing, and shaking her head, she turned to step back into the cubicle. 'If you don't want to listen to me,' she began, a tremor evident in her voice, and with a groan, he tried to grasp the robe to stop her. But his strength was greater than hers, and he felt her grip give way. Almost without his volition, the robe slipped off her shoulders and into his hands, and he was left staring at her with eyes as dark as burnt sugar mirroring his frustrations.

'For God's sake!' he muttered savagely, thrusting the bathrobe back at her, but Jordan didn't take it. It fell to the floor, just inside the shower cubicle, and Rhys was no longer capable of controlling his hungry gaze. His eyes moved irresistibly over her body, lingering longest on the rosy dark crests of her breasts, and the tantalising glimpse of her womanhood, before he noticed the faint pink blemishes visible in the white skin previously hidden by her bikini.

His eyes moved to her face, and as if sensing his enquiry, she touched her hip selfconsciously. 'German measles,' she said, with evident reluctance. 'Karen got it, and I got it too. That's why I haven't seen you. I asked Daddy to phone you, but he wouldn't, and it was only today I learned from Raoul that you'd phoned me . . .'

'Oh, Jordan!' With a groan he reached for her, and hauling her trembling body against him, found her eager mouth with his. Her lips parted instinctively, and the pounding in Rhys's head surged to a crescendo as her arms wound themselves about him.

She moulded her body to his, making him overpoweringly aware of how uncomfortable tight pants could be in a situation like this, but the feel of her skin was like silk. His hands slid down her back, finding the rounded curve of her rear and urging her

even closer, the sensual excitement of her nearness
arousing a physical ache inside him.

His mouth possessed hers seeking its own satisfaction, and with his mouth still on hers, he swung her up
into his arms and carried her into his bedroom.

'My hair . . .' she protested, as he lowered her on to
the bed, but his: 'Don't worry,' seemed to satisfy her,
and in any case she was loath to let him go.

The bed was soft, the bedroom blessedly cool, the
pale green satin bedspread like a backcloth to her
golden beauty. Jordan rolled restlessly upon its silken
covers as he tore off his shirt and pants, and then he
was beside her, gathering her warmth and sensuality
into his arms.

He knew she was a virgin, and although his
conscience stirred at what he was about to do, it was
quickly squashed. He wanted her; she wanted him; it
was as simple as that. And he could no more have
resisted her than the moon could resist following its
sister sun into the heavens.

And it was heavenly. In spite of her inexperience,
Jordan was more than ready for him, and the initial
opposition he encountered soon gave way beneath his
persuasive assault. But it was all over much too soon.
He had wanted to take his time, to savour every inch
of her enchanting body, but his own body's needs had
overwhelmed him, and Jordan shifted protestingly
beneath his sudden prostration.

'I'm sorry,' he muttered, a rueful smile lifting the
corners of his mouth, but she was not placated.

'Why did you stop?' she breathed, as his tongue
stroked sensuously over one taut nipple. 'Oh, Rhys,
don't move. I don't want you to. Just stay where you
are, please . . .'

'Oh, love,' his lips parted, 'I'm not going anywhere,
honestly.' His mouth caressed her midriff as he slid

down her body, and by the time he returned to her mouth, she was weak and clinging to him. This time she moved with him, experiencing the same fulfilling peak of ecstasy that left them both emotionally—and physically—satiated . . .

It has always been like that with them, he remembered broodingly. No matter how often he made love to Jordan, he always wanted more, and in the aftermath of the rift their relationship caused with her father, she was more often at his house than at the hotel.

Of course, their association was looked on with disapproval by almost all the Lucas's friends, the older members of the community siding with her father, and the younger ones too consumed with envy to defend Jordan.

Not that she seemed to care. What other people thought of their relationship did not concern her, and Rhys had found himself refusing concerts and performing engagements just so that he did not have to leave the island. His agent and manager were not at all happy with his attitude. Bernie Withers, the man who had discovered him singing in a wine bar in Chelsea and offered him his first recording contract, had flown out to Eleutha twice in an attempt to get him to change his mind, but they had been wasted journeys. Rhys wasn't interested in making more money. He had more than enough to live on, and Bernie's warnings that the public would soon find themselves a new idol to worship had fallen on deaf ears. And then Jennifer had arrived, bringing Lucy with her, and everything had fallen apart.

He had often wondered how Jennifer had discovered where he was living. He certainly hadn't left any clues, and apart from the other members of the band and their girl-friends, and Bernie, of course, there was no

one else. But at the time, her appearance had
overridden all other considerations, and Jordan's
reaction had been as violent as his own.

If only she had been prepared to listen to him, he
reflected bitterly, sliding his fingers into the sand. But
no matter how he had tried to justify his actions, she
had spurned his excuses, and the evidence had been
tipped heavily against him.

He gazed moodily towards the distant horizon, feeling
the tight ball of frustration expanding inside him. God
knew, he had put all this behind him long ago, so why
was he resurrecting it now? From the moment he
accepted responsibility for Lucy, he had damned
himself in Jordan's eyes, and if she hadn't believed him
then, she sure as hell wouldn't believe him now!

'What are you thinking, Daddy?'

Lucy's slim form blocked his view suddenly, and he
looked up to find her gazing down at him with evident
concern. Forcing a smile to his lips, he got lithely to
his feet, and ignoring her troubled expression, he
slipped a casual arm about her shoulders.

'How do you fancy going back to Nassau?' he asked
lightly, seizing the excuse to escape. 'You'd certainly
have more entertainment there, and plenty of people
your own age to have fun with. You must be bored
here, with nothing to do and nowhere to go.'

'Are you bored, Daddy?'

Lucy looked up at him anxiously, and realising it
was a double-edged question, Rhys temporised. 'I'm
not sixteen,' he responded, as they began to walk back
to the house.

'And I'm not bored,' declared Lucy firmly. 'I don't
want to go back to Nassau, Daddy. I don't want to
share you with a lot of other people.'

'Okay.' Rhys despised the faint feeling of relief her
words engendered. 'So we'll stay here.'

'You don't mind?'

'Why should I mind?' he exclaimed, with determined optimism. 'I wanted to come. It was my decision.'

Lucy sighed, resting her head against his shoulder. 'I just don't want you to be unhappy, Daddy.'

'Unhappy?' Rhys glanced down at her. 'Since when has my happiness come into this?'

'Since this morning,' confessed Lucy, avoiding his eyes. 'Jordan Lucas is—quite attractive, isn't she?'

Rhys stiffened. 'Jordan Lucas?'

'Hmm.' Lucy drew away from him to mount the verandah steps, and Rhys was grateful for the momentary chance to recover his detachment. 'I saw you looking at her this morning.' She paused, then turned to look at him. 'Are you in love with her?'

CHAPTER NINE

It was another week before Jordan encountered Rhys again.

During that time she managed to convince herself that her visit to the house at Planter's Point had not been the disaster she had at first thought it. After all, it had enabled her to look at her relationship with Rhys more objectively, and his behaviour had confirmed that she had been right about him all along.

The night he called at the hotel, she had blamed herself for the angry words which had been spoken. Her own attitude had initiated the row which had ensued, and that was why, after a sleepless night, she had driven out to his house to apologise. Besides which, she had wanted to absolve herself of any responsibility for his future actions, and to begin with she had thought she had handled it rather well.

It hadn't been easy for her going to his home. The place held so many painful memories, and the sight of him swimming with his daughter had evoked unwelcome images of the past. But Rhys had been polite, and she had been reassured, and only when Lucy came on the scene did the atmosphere deteriorate. Perhaps she shouldn't have spoken of Neil. It was true enough that he wanted to marry her. He had spoken of it on numerous occasions. But it was not true that she was considering it; at least, not in the near future. Neil understood that she needed time before committing herself completely, and until Lucy asked her question she had had no intention of discussing her future.

It had been a defensive reflex, a need to justify her unmarried state to a girl to whom, no doubt, she was an object of contempt. If Rhys had told his daughter about their relationship it could only have been in the most uncomplimentary terms, and she had resented Lucy's deliberate attempt to disconcert her.

Even so, she had never anticipated Rhys might react in the way he had. The inner flesh of her lips was still sore from his bruising assault, and her fingertips tingled from their unwilling contact with the hair-roughened skin of his chest. He must love his daughter very much, she thought bitterly, refusing to analyse the unwelcome surge of emotion that churned inside her. How could she believe otherwise, when he had accepted full responsibility for Lucy after Jennifer had been killed?

The invitation to the Hammonds' barbecue came during the following week, and although Jordan was tempted to refuse, for once Neil took the upper hand.

'Look, if you don't go, Cilla will think it's because you're afraid to meet Rhys Williams again,' he declared one morning, coming over to the hotel to take her riding. Neil kept a small stable of horses at Coral Cay, and he and Jordan occasionally enjoyed a gallop along the beach to Thunder Cove. 'You realise she'll be inviting him, don't you? I imagine that's the main reason she's holding it. He's due to leave in a week or so, isn't he?'

'Is he?' Jordan tried to sound uninterested, and Neil gave her an impatient look.

'Don't you know? You've spoken to him, haven't you? Raoul tells me he came to the hotel for dinner one evening.'

'Raoul is an old gossip!' declared Jordan tautly, making a mental note to speak to him next time she had an opportunity. She tucked her foot into the

stirrup of the mare he had brought for her to ride, and
swung herself up on to its back. 'As a matter of fact,
he and his daughter did come to the hotel one evening.
It was the night you were in Galveston, actually. But
they didn't stay long. Just—just for a drink.'

'And?'

'And?' Jordan dug her heels into the mare's sides
and urged the docile animal forward, threading her way
between the trees to the beach. 'And what?' she called
back over her shoulder, and Neil came cantering after
her.

'What did he say?' he asked, keeping pace with her.
'Was he civil?'

'Oh—yes.' Jordan was glad of the exertion to
account for the sudden colour in her cheeks. 'Of
course.'

'Why of course? I thought you didn't exactly part
on the best of terms?'

'That was ten years ago, Neil,' Jordan protested
quickly.

'So you'll come to the barbecue with me?'

Jordan sighed, cornered. 'If you really want me to.'

'I really want you to,' he averred, reaching across to
cover her hand where it lay on her thigh. 'I'll tell
Cilla. She'll be delighted.'

Jordan suspected this was true. Cilla Hammond's
social gatherings were not known for their excitement,
but with the possibility of Rhys Williams being in
attendance, and Jordan roped in, too, she could look
forward to an interesting evening at least.

For her part, Jordan suffered a variety of reactions,
the most frequent being the conviction that she should
have found some excuse to refuse. If Rhys did turn
up, it would all be horribly embarrassing, and she
would feel like a specimen under a microscope,
providing entertainment for the other guests present.

But after what she had said, she could hardly broach the subject with Neil, and eventually she gave up the idea of bunking and put her mind to the question of what she was going to wear.

For a beach barbecue, formal clothes were obviously out, and the choice seemed to lie between trousers and a shirt or a skirt and tank top. Neil had also suggested she wear her bathing suit under whatever garment she decided upon, but as she had no intention of exposing herself in front of Rhys, Jordan intended to ignore this particular piece of advice.

Karen, however, had her own opinion. 'You can't wear those slacks and that shirt for a party!' she exclaimed, coming into her sister's bedroom as Jordan was getting ready for her date. 'At least wear something feminine, Jordan! Don't put yourself down! Show him what he's lost!'

Jordan heaved a sigh. 'I suppose you mean Rhys Williams,' she exclaimed, pausing in the process of buttoning up her shirt, and Karen nodded.

'Who else? I wouldn't let him see me looking like a drag. I'd make him so jealous of Neil, he'd want to knock his teeth in!'

Jordan uttered a nervous laugh. 'You're crazy.'

'No. Only human,' responded Karen drily. 'Are you really going like that? Or are you going to shock the lot of them?'

Jordan shook her head. 'How could I shock anyone?'

'How could you——' Karen broke off impatiently. 'Jordan, don't be silly. You know you're good to look at. Okay, you're slim, but that's fashionable these days. If you stopped living on your nerves so much, perhaps you'd even gain some weight. In any case, you've got it where it matters. You've always had nice breasts.'

'Karen!'

'Well, it's true.' Karen looked down at her own small bosom resignedly. 'I've always envied you. But as long as I can remember you've made no effort to take advantage of your appearance.'

Jordan bent her head. 'No, well——'

'I know, I know,' Karen swiftly placated her. 'You've always been too busy. But tonight—now—take my advice and wear something else. And let me do your hair for once.'

Jordan hesitated. 'What else could I wear? The dresses I have are either too formal or too old. I could wear the skirt and blouse I wore to dine at Neil's a couple of weeks ago, but I thought a change was in order.'

'It is.' Karen whirled about. 'Wait here, I won't be a minute.'

When she came back, she was carrying a white cotton voile smock and a black suede belt that fastened with cords. 'There you are,' she said, tossing the smock on to the bed. 'Try that on. I haven't worn it yet, and it should suit you.'

Jordan hesitated. 'You mean—wear it with these trousers?' she ventured, looking down at her white slacks, but Karen quickly shook her head.

'Try it on,' she suggested, helping Jordan to unfasten her shirt and pants. 'Hurry up, or we won't have time to do your hair. And you're not going out with it looking like that.'

'What's wrong with my hair?' exclaimed Jordan, observing the coiled rope at her nape without satisfaction. 'You know, perhaps I should have it cut. It would be so much easier to manage if it was short.'

'Forget it,' said Karen, picking up the smock and slipping it over her sister's head. 'There, it's long enough. I thought it would be. Here, tie the belt and let me look at you.'

Jordan caught her breath as she saw her reflection in the wardrobe mirror. The loose voile smock reached scarcely to her knees, and when she tied the belt about her waist, it lifted it a further inch at least. In addition to which, although the sleeves were elbow length and full, the neckline dipped alarmingly, and there were no convenient buttons to hide the dusky hollow just visible between her breasts.

'I can't wear this!' she exclaimed, staring at her image helplessly, but Karen was fervently enthusiastic.

'Of course you can,' she declared, surveying her sister's slim brown legs, now attractively exposed, with approval. 'You look great, Jordan, honestly. With your tan, it looks fantastic! Forget about Rhys Williams. Neil will have a fit!'

'That's what I'm afraid of,' sighed Jordan worriedly, but it wasn't completely true. Her mind persisted in picturing Rhys's reactions when he saw her in something so revealing, and although she wanted to dismiss it, the temptation to shock him was there.

'Oh, Jordan, stop looking so doubtful!' Karen put her hands on her hips and surveyed the other girl critically. 'You really do look smashing. And you can wear your bikini underneath without feeling far too hot.'

Jordan sighed. 'I wasn't going to wear a bikini.'

'Why not? It's a beach party, isn't it?'

'Well, yes——'

'There you are, then. Didn't Neil suggest it? After all that sand, you'll be glad of a swim, believe me. And you'll feel out of it if you can't participate.'

Jordan caught her lower lip between her teeth. 'It's awfully short.'

'It's fashionable,' said Karen again. 'Honestly, love, you'll knock them dead! They've grown so used to seeing you looking like a woman twice your age, they'll hardly recognise you.'

Thirty minutes later, Jordan realised the truth of Karen's statement when Neil failed to recognise her as she crossed the lobby. He was in his usual place, propped against the reception desk talking to Raoul, and he scarcely paid any attention to the slim young woman, dressed in white, who came across the sun-warmed tiles on high heels. With her hair unbound for once, and simply secured at her nape with a leather thong, she didn't look much like the Jordan he was used to seeing, and when the several gold bracelets she was wearing on her wrist rattled on the desk beside him, he turned with some impatience to meet her troubled gaze.

'My God, *Jordan*!' he exclaimed, his astonishment seeming to confirm her worst fears. But then, to confound her suspicions, he added: 'You look terrific! What happened to you?'

'You really think I look all right?' she asked, aware that Raoul was staring at her too with a mixture of admiration and disbelief, and Neil nodded.

'You—well, you always look good to me, Jordan, you know that,' he said, belatedly qualifying his reaction. 'But tonight you're something special. Really, you look beautiful!'

Jordan coloured. 'You're sure this short skirt is quite decent?'

'Hey, you've got good legs, why not show them?' Neil declared firmly. 'Come on, let's go. I can't wait to see Cilla's face when she sees you. And Martina, too. I hear she's home for a holiday.'

Martina Hammond was Cilla's daughter, and briefly Jordan's heart sank. She and Martina had never been the best of friends, and although they were much of an age, they had little in common. Martina had gone to

college in the United States, and after several minor
setbacks had succeeded in wedding one of the most
eligible Senators in the country. The fact that the
marriage had foundered after only two years was not
considered a failure on Martina's part. On the
contrary, she used the contacts she had made to make
a very satisfactory career for herself in television, and
these days she could be seen as anchor-person on a
west coast news programme. No doubt, the fact that
Rhys Williams was staying on Eleutha at the moment
had attracted her back to the island, thought Jordan
cynically. If Martina succeeded in filming an interview
with Rhys, who these days avoided that kind of
publicity, she would certainly be applauded by her
sponsors.

The drive to the Hammonds' home took a little over
twenty minutes. Like Rhys's house, it was situated on
the east side of the island, and below the sprawling
colonial-style dwelling, which had been on this spot in
one form or another since the eighteenth century, a
small, private cove was sheltered by palms and
flowering casuarinas. The Hammond family had lived
on the island for over two hundred years, although
these days Paul Hammond could not rely on the
traditional crops of pineapple and sugar cane to
sustain his wealth. Like his daughter, he spent much
time in the United States, only coming back for
prolonged visits when the weather there defeated him.

Tonight there were several cars parked in the drive
leading to the house, and Jordan recognised most of
them. There were still a number of families living on
the island, and her father had always maintained that
so long as they kept a nucleus of wealthy settlers,
Eleutha would not suffer the commercialisation of
some of the other islands. He was probably right, she
reflected. She and Neil were the outsiders here, in that

they made their living from tourism. But in her experience it was not tourists who spoiled their natural resources. It was the speculators who moved in and invested money in huge leisure complexes, instead of allowing the local economy to develop at its own pace.

Neil parked his car in a vacant space, and he and Jordan walked the length of the drive to where a string of coloured lights illuminated the terrace. Jordan looked rather anxiously for the familiar jeep, but it was not in evidence, and she breathed a little more easily as they reached the throng of guests already gathered around the swimming pool. Down on the beach, fires had been lighted, and the appetising aroma of steaks grilling over charcoal drifted irresistibly on the breeze. But the Hammonds' guests were presently employed in the interesting business of renewing acquaintances, and Jordan and Neil were swiftly gathered into their midst.

'How—charming you look, Jordan,' Cilla Hammond declared, with deliberate hesitation. In a loose-fitting caftan of embroidered silk, Cilla herself looked rather overdressed, and Jordan withstood the inevitable comparison easily, refusing to be perturbed.

'You look ravishing, my dear,' Paul Hammond assured her warmly, bestowing an affectionate kiss on each cheek. 'Take no notice of Cilla. She's only jealous. She doesn't care for fluffy ducklings who suddenly turn out to be swans.'

'Is that what I am, Paul?' Jordan countered smilingly, and he looked to Neil for confirmation.

'Wouldn't you say so, old man?' he exclaimed. 'I always knew that some day she'd come out of her shell.'

'I think you're mixing your metaphors, Paul,' responded Neil, with a chuckle. 'You must have been sampling this punch before we arrived!'

'Well, what's the use of making the damn stuff if you can't enjoy it,' responded Paul vehemently. 'What do you think of it, Jordan? Here, have another glass.'

'Do you want to make me drunk?' protested Jordan, laughing in spite of herself. It was good to relax, and the realisation that Rhys was not here had done wonders for her confidence. 'I haven't finished this one yet.'

Paul grunted and moved away to attend to his other guests, and Neil bent his head to hers. 'Here comes Martina,' he murmured, nodding towards the house, and Jordan turned her head to see the Hammonds' daughter making her way in their direction.

In transparent harem pants and a matching silvery tunic, the other girl looked svelte and sophisticated, and Jordan's composure faltered. Martina looked every inch the successful woman she was, and her smile wavered only slightly when she glimpsed Jordan's slim brown figure.

'I knew you'd come, Jordan,' she exclaimed, hugging the other girl with what Jordan herself felt to be rather doubtful sincerity. 'Neil.' She nodded to Jordan's companion. 'As soon as Mummy told me she was inviting Rhys Williams, I felt convinced you wouldn't let us down. I mean,' she paused to let her words sink in, 'that affair between you two is old history now, isn't it? It's so much more civilised to be able to put the past behind you.'

Jordan had stiffened, and as if sensing her reaction, Neil put a reassuring arm about her waist. 'Williams is here?' he asked casually, and Martina smiled.

'Of course. He and I went swimming earlier. He's upstairs now, getting changed. Haven't you seen Lucy? His daughter, you know? She's about here somewhere, though I'm not sure where.'

Having delivered her bombshell, Martina drifted off to speak to her mother, and Neil looked down at Jordan with unconcealed impatience. 'She really enjoyed that, didn't she?' he muttered, touching Jordan's cheek. 'Trust Martina to make the most of her opportunities! She probably sees Williams as a possible candidate for her next *in-depth* special.'

'Hmm.' Jordan tried to sound as if she agreed with him, but privately she had other ideas. A woman like Martina could not be unaware of Rhys's other qualities, and her motives for informing Jordan of their relationship had not been simply to express a commercial interest. She found him attractive; most women did; and her reminder of their *past* association had been intended as a warning.

'You're not worried because he's here, are you?' Neil asked now, putting a hand at either side of her waist and turning her towards him.

'No!' Jordan's response was a little too hasty, but Neil didn't seem to notice.

'Good,' he murmured, lowering his cheek to her hair. 'Let me handle Rhys Williams, if he starts annoying you.'

Jordan was grateful for Neil's support, but she couldn't help the unwilling thought that in any confrontation between them, he was likely to come off the loser. He might be as tall as Rhys, and broader, but he did not have Rhys's athletic litheness, or the street-wise experience that eighteen years of fending for himself had afforded. He was a big man, but he was not tough, and Jordan wondered if he had any idea how ruthless Rhys could be.

As she thought of this, her fingers went automatically to her lips, seeking and finding the tender inner curve that still bore the scars of Rhys's assault. Damn him, she thought frustratedly, why had he come here tonight, when in the past he had invariably refused all invitations? And as she pondered this enigma, she saw Lucy, seated sullenly in a corner of the verandah, watching her.

CHAPTER TEN

THE girl was alone, and judging by her expression, she was not enjoying herself at all. She had a glass of Coke balanced on the knee of her jeans, and when Jordan intercepted her brooding glance, she immediately bent her head to sip from the straw that protruded from it. But as soon as Jordan pretended to look away, Lucy's head came up again, and although she had no reason to like the girl, she couldn't help feeling sorry for her.

Excusing herself to Neil, who had been captured in conversation by the island doctor and his wife, Jordan crossed the tiles surrounding the pool, and mounted the steps to the verandah. 'Hello, Lucy,' she said, refusing to be deterred by the girl's sulky demeanour, and Lucy was forced to answer her or ignore her altogether.

She was too young—and too unsure of herself in her present setting—to do the latter, and lifting a careless shoulder, she murmured: 'Hi,' in an offhand tone.

'I didn't know you were here,' added Jordan, waving the glass of punch in her hand. 'After a few more of these, nobody will know who's here. Have you tasted the stuff? It's lethal!'

Lucy pursed her lips. 'I've got Coke,' she said flatly, and Jordan had to think again.

'Have you been swimming?' she asked, broaching the only subject which she thought might bring some reaction from the girl, and Lucy looked up at her resentfully.

'No.'

'Oh!' Jordan had already guessed this was the case. 'Well, I expect you will later. Haven't you been introduced to any of the other young people yet?'

'I don't want to meet any of the other young people,' retorted Lucy shortly. 'I told Daddy I'd rather stay with him, but——'

She broke off abruptly, and Jordan couldn't help herself from prompting: 'But—what?'

Lucy hunched her shoulders. 'Nothing.'

Jordan sighed. 'All right. So come and join us.'

'No.' Lucy hesitated a moment and then she gave an unwilling grimace. 'I mean—no, thanks,' she added grudgingly. 'I'll wait for Daddy.'

Jordan hesitated. 'If you're sure . . .'

Lucy looked up. 'Thanks anyway,' she appended. 'You're a lot nicer than I thought. Better than Miss Hammond anyway.'

Jordan's lips parted. 'Thanks!'

'I mean it.' Lucy sniffed. 'She's a vampire. I've seen women like her before. Daddy usually recognises the type, too, only tonight he wouldn't listen to me.'

Noticing Neil was threading his way through the throng to reach her, Jordan realised with some regret that their conversation was about to be curtailed. 'Are you sure you want to stay here——' she began, only to suspend her speech abruptly when the screen door behind Lucy opened and Rhys himself emerged.

His timing was perfect, she thought irrelevantly, coinciding as it did with her escort's arrival at the steps. Neil came up on to the verandah as Rhys closed the screen door behind him, and Jordan felt Neil's hand upon her shoulder, like a blatant display of his possession.

Rhys's hair was still damp from his swim, and as it had grown in the weeks since he came to the island, it now brushed the neckline of his short-sleeved sweat shirt. Unlike Neil, who was wearing shorts, Rhys wore trousers—white cotton pants, that clung to his lean body like a second skin, moulding his hips and outlining the powerful muscles of his thighs. And because his feet were bare, he had folded back the cuffs to halfway up his calves.

Jordan was intensely aware of him, aware of his eyes upon her, noting the daring dip of her neckline, the long length of legs exposed by the smock, and the sensual beauty of her hair, loose down her back. But she was also aware of Neil's antipathy as he stood there, stiff beside her, and his unmistakable resentment at Rhys's insolent appraisal.

'Jordan,' Rhys murmured now, inclining his head towards her, and taking a deep breath, she turned to Neil.

'Do you know Rhys Williams?' she asked, although she knew full well he didn't. 'And his daughter, Lucy.' She paused. 'This is—this is Neil Ferris, Rhys. The owner of the Coral Cay Hotel.'

'Ferris.'

Rhys made no effort to shake hands, and the two men stood staring at one another, as if measuring the other's capabilities. Beside Neil, Rhys had the rapier-thinness of a Toledo blade, and like the weapon he represented, Jordan thought he looked quite as dangerous.

'I've been talking to Miss Lucas, Daddy,' declared Lucy suddenly, breaking the ominous silence which had fallen on their small gathering. 'She asked me if I'd like to join them, but I told her I was waiting for you.'

'Did you?' Rhys's hand slid affectionately over his

daughter's shoulder, and watching those brown fingers, dark against Lucy's much fairer skin, Jordan felt a shivery feeling deep down in her stomach. 'That was kind of you, Jordan,' he added, ensnaring her with his tawny gaze. 'Remind me to thank you later.'

Later?

Jordan guessed that like her Neil had taken note of Rhys's deliberately provocative statement, and the contraction of his hand against her shoulder seemed to confirm it. 'There's no need to thank me,' she replied hastily, giving Lucy the benefit of a forced smile. 'You'll be all right now, won't you, Lucy? I'm sure your father won't abandon you again.'

She felt, rather than saw, the hostility her words had evoked from Rhys, but happily Lucy seemed unaffected by the undercurrents in the conversation. 'I'll see he doesn't,' she exclaimed, capturing his hand in hers and holding it to her cheek. She looked up at her father adoringly. 'Let's get some punch, shall we? Miss Lucas says it's really something.'

'Please—call me Jordan,' said Jordan, half wishing she had not given in to the impulse to be bitchy. 'Let's all get some punch.' She looked hopefully up at Neil. 'The smell of food is making me hungry.'

To her relief, Neil allowed himself to be nudged down the verandah steps again and across the tiled area to the buffet tables. A glance over her shoulder had assured Jordan that although Rhys and Lucy were following, there was a comfortable space between them, and after collecting fresh glasses, she was quite willing to allow Neil to draw her away from the throng. But her hope that the incident with Rhys was over was shortlived.

'It's just as well we split up when we did,' Neil muttered, his aggressive tone tempered somewhat by the piped music issuing from the loudspeakers set at either end of the verandah. 'That fellow really got my goat, speaking to you like that. Bloody insolence! Who the hell does he think he is?'

Jordan sighed. 'Oh, Neil——'

'Don't try to defend him to me! The fellow's a barbarian, anyone can see that. What I don't understand is, why you felt the need to go and console his daughter! For heaven's sake, she's not a babe in arms. She must be well used to her father's behaviour by now.'

'Does it matter?' Jordan sipped nervously at the punch in her glass, hoping no one else was listening to them. 'I felt sorry for Lucy, that's all. And you were talking to the Chesneys . . .'

'Yes, I was.' Neil took a mouthful of his own drink, and then, with a shrug, he determinedly cast off his ill humour. 'Okay, so I was neglecting you. I'm sorry.' He bent to touch her temple with his lips. 'I promise I won't leave your side again tonight.'

It should have been what she wanted to hear—it *was* what she wanted to hear, Jordan told herself severely—but that didn't prevent her eyes from straying in Rhys's direction when his appearance aroused the usual response from the other guests. As Jordan and Neil stood to one side, each endeavouring to ignore what was going on, Martina Hammond drew Rhys into the limelight, and the genuine warmth of his welcome was difficult to disregard.

'You will sing for us later, won't you, Rhys?' Cilla Hammond exclaimed confidently, only to look decidedly put out when he politely declined the invitation.

'Rhys doesn't do that sort of thing, Mother,' Martina protested half impatiently. Then to Rhys: 'Except in very special circumstances. Or if someone special asked him.' She paused, then added softly: 'Would you sing if I asked you?'

'Not even for you, Martina,' Rhys responded firmly, and Jordan saw Lucy, clinging to his arm, look up at him delightedly. 'I'm sorry, I didn't bring my guitar to the party.'

Martina pouted. 'But couldn't I persuade you?' she persisted, ignoring Lucy's triumphant expression. 'I do have a guitar you could borrow.'

'I don't sing unless I'm being paid for it,' replied Rhys shortly, deliberately alienating the majority of the Hammonds' guests with a statement Jordan knew to be false. 'I'm on holiday, Martina. Now excuse me. I left my shoes around here somewhere.'

Neil, who had listened to what was going on with a taut expression, now expelled the air in his lungs in an angry breath. 'Isn't that just typical!' he snarled, his lips curling. 'That's how he repays the Hammonds' hospitality in inviting him here. I tell you, the fellow's a barbarian. He hasn't got the manners of a pig!'

Jordan bent her head. 'It's not true, you know,' she said unwillingly, and Neil stared at her.

'What's not true? That Williams has no manners? Of course it's true. I——

'No.' Jordan sighed. 'I meant about him not singing unless he's paid for it.' She moistened her lips. 'He does. Often. I—oh, he does quite a lot of concerts in aid of children's charities, that sort of thing.' She coloured. 'I've read about them in the newspapers.'

Neil's features hardened. 'Really?'

'Yes, really.' Jordan took a deep breath.

'And you feel you have to defend him?' Neil enquired tautly. 'Is that right?'

Jordan shook her head. 'I just didn't think it was fair that you should get the wrong impression about him.'

'Oh, I haven't got the wrong impression,' retorted Neil harshly. 'Williams knows exactly what he's doing. He knew the Hammonds would expect him to perform so he deliberately chooses not to. Who was it who said there was no such thing as bad publicity? He doesn't care what these people think about him. Just so long as they don't forget who he is.'

Jordan caught her lower lip between her teeth. She was unwillingly aware that Neil's attitude was not entirely unbiased, and while she wanted to agree with him, honesty prevented her from doing so. Rhys wasn't like that. He wouldn't simply refuse to sing because he enjoyed embarrassing the Hammonds. She didn't know why she was so certain of that, but she was. It was far more likely that he found the invitation unacceptable because he had hoped to escape from his public image, and Martina's attempt to back him into a corner was not a situation he would condone. Martina should not have asked him, Jordan acknowledged silently, squashing the disturbing memories of the way Rhys had once sung for her . . .

With some relief she noticed that the other guests were dispersing from the area around the swimming pool and making their way down to the beach. Evidently Rhys's refusal to respond to Martina's pleas was not to be allowed to disrupt the rest of the evening, and Rhys and Lucy had both disappeared into the shadows beyond the terrace.

'Let's go and get ourselves a steak,' suggested Neil,

finishing his punch and depositing Jordan's empty glass along with his own. 'Who cares what Rhys Williams does or doesn't do? You're right—it's not worth bothering about.'

This wasn't exactly what Jordan had said, but she was quite willing to abandon that particular topic of conversation. 'The food does smell delicious,' she exclaimed, with an effort, aware that her appetite had suffered along with her conscience. 'Oh, look—they've hired a steel band, too.' She pointed to the gleam of the metal instruments being set up on the sand. 'How exciting!'

'And more appealing than that trashy stuff Williams plays,' added Neil, unable to resist the taunting comparison.

Jordan made no response to his derisive words, simply going ahead of him down the steps, taking off her sandals as her feet encountered the soft sand. Leaving the sandals on the steps, she trod lightly across to the torchlit area surrounding the barbecue fires, and accepted a plate from Paul Hammond and a thick wedge of steak from his steward.

Neil followed, and fortunately there was no further opportunity for private conversation as other members of the party surrounded them. The food, the quality of the wine, and the abilities of the steel band took precedence over everything else, and Jordan was happy to make up the numbers without actually taking an active part. She noticed Neil had been cornered by the Chesneys' daughter, Joanna, who was presently on holiday from the nursing post she held at a hospital in Miami, and was grateful. It meant he wouldn't notice how little she was eating, Jordan reflected thankfully. She had no wish for him to start suspecting her defence of Rhys Williams had been anything more than a desire for fair play.

'All alone?'

The voice that had always had the power to stir the downy hairs of her spine spoke softly from behind her, and Jordan did not have to turn to feel his dark, disturbing magnetism. But turn she did, if only to assure herself that Lucy was beside him, and then knew a sense of dismay when she found that he was on his own.

'I—where's your daughter?' she exclaimed, looking past him to avoid looking into those brilliant tawny eyes, and he raised the glass he was carrying to his lips and looked at her over the rim.

'She's dancing,' he said, nodding to where some of the younger guests were gyrating to the rhythm of the steel band. 'Martina asked a boy called Steve Mallory to look after her, and he was persuasive enough to get her to join them.'

'Steve Mallory.' Jordan nodded politely. 'His father runs the importing company in town. I believe he's at school in England for most of the year.'

'Is that right?' Rhys absorbed the information. 'Well, you'd know that better than me.'

'Yes, I would.' Jordan pushed the steak round on her plate, wishing she felt more hungry. 'Er—where is Martina? She told us you and she had been swimming earlier.'

Rhys bent his head. 'There was quite a group of us,' he conceded flatly. 'Martina; her father; Joanna Chesney; and several others I can't remember the names of.'

'I see.' Jordan knew an unwarranted lightening of her spirits. 'I—your hair's still wet.'

'But drying fast,' he assured her levelly. 'Want to feel it?'

Her colour rose. 'Of course not.'

Rhys shrugged. 'I see you're wearing your hair loose. Is that for the boy-friend?'

'Um—Neil likes it loose, yes.' Jordan moistened her lips. 'It was Karen's idea, as a matter of fact.'

'That girl has sense,' remarked Rhys drily. He paused, then added: 'Are you trying to eat that steak, or play games with it?'

Jordan's hand trembled, and she lifted her other hand to steady the plate. 'I'm not very hungry,' she said tightly. 'And it was a very large piece of meat. I—er—I'll get rid of it.'

'Let me.' Rhys took the plate out of her hands and after tossing the meat on to the sand, he dropped the plate into the container provided for the purpose. Then he rescued two glasses of wine from a passing attendant, and handed one to Jordan. 'Less difficult to get rid of,' he essayed sardonically.

Jordan looked behind her doubtfully. 'You shouldn't throw meat on to the sand,' she protested.

'Why not? Let the seabirds have a feast,' he retorted carelessly. 'Do you have any idea how many dead bodies are disposed of that way?'

Jordan looked down into her glass. 'I'd rather not talk about such things.'

'Okay.' Rhys sounded indifferent. 'Let's talk about you. You look beautiful tonight.' His voice had thickened slightly. 'Has your boy-friend told you that?'

Jordan glanced around, half afraid that their conversation could be heard but happily the shadows around the barbecue tables concealed them from too many interested eyes. And besides, most people seemed intent on enjoying the food and with the wine flowing freely there was a constant buzz of voices to compete with the music.

'I think I ought to go and find Neil,' she said now, edging away from him, but Rhys's hand closed round her wrist, preventing her. Without her volition, his hand slid down into hers, the fingers separating hers and pushing between them. In seconds, her hand was enfolded, the hard warmth of his palm pressed against hers, and her breathing quickened uncontrollably as she looked up into his tense face. 'Rhys——'

'Let's go for a walk,' he said huskily, his eyes on her parted lips, and Jordan's skin feathered with goose-bumps. 'I want to talk to you,' he added, 'without the benefit of an audience. No one will miss us, not just for fifteen minutes.'

Jordan dug her toes into the sand. 'Ha-have you been drinking, Rhys?' she demanded in a low voice. 'You know I can't go with you. I don't really know how you have the nerve to ask me after what you did! I can only assume it's Paul's punch that's responsible for this sudden bravado. Please let go of me. Neil's looking for me.'

'To hell with Neil!' said Rhys almost inaudibly. 'Okay—yes, I have been drinking. Why else would I expect human behaviour from you?'

'That's a foul thing to say!' exclaimed Jordan, dragging her hand out of his grasp, and he let it go.

'But apt, don't you think?' he countered harshly, and without another word, he stalked away.

By the time Neil did come looking for her, Jordan had herself in control again, and she was able to reply to his apologies without embarrassment. She assured him that she had not felt neglected in his absence, and Neil glanced ruefully over his shoulder.

'You know, Jo and I were once quite close,' he admitted, with a grimace. 'We're about the same age, and when we were kids, we were always together.'

Jordan listened with interest, realising as she did so that she felt no twinge of jealousy at his words. And she should, she thought impatiently. If she cared about Neil, she should feel something when he was telling her he had just spent the best part of an hour with a girl he had once been close to.

'She seems a nice girl,' she commented now, and Neil nodded. Then he slipped his arm about her.

'Not as nice as you,' he whispered, touching her temple with his lips, and Jordan was angry with herself for the feeling of revulsion his tender caress evoked.

Fortunately, the food was being cleared away now, and more of the guests were taking to the impromptu dance floor. The damp sand near the water's edge was springy under their feet, and Jordan joined in determinedly when Neil led her out to participate.

It should have been an enjoyable evening, but it wasn't. Jordan found her eyes wandering restlessly over the other guests, unconsciously searching for Rhys's lean frame, and when she did see him standing by the buffet table, her feet refused to obey her and she almost tripped. The fact that he was alone made her that much more selfconscious, and she wondered where Martina was and whether Rhys's earlier recalcitrance had soured their relationship.

Lucy, at least, seemed to be having a good time. Steve Mallory was a nice boy, and he had evidently no objection to being appointed her escort for the evening. An appropriate choice, thought Jordan bitterly. She couldn't believe Martina had had no hand in the most attractive youth present being employed to distract Lucy's attention from her father.

It was a warm evening and gradually people began to drift away from the music in favour of cooler pursuits. In two and threes, they disappeared in the direction of the changing cabins situated beside the swimming pool, reappearing minutes later in trunks or bikinis. Their voices echoed shrilly as they splashed into the ocean, and Neil turned to watch them, smiling at their antics.

'Shall we join them?' he suggested, gripping her forearms and holding her in front of him, and Jordan moistened her lips.

'I don't know . . .' she began, not terribly eager to participate in the improvised game of water polo some of the guests had struck up, but Neil was enthusiastic and she didn't like to disappoint him. 'Maybe later,' she evaded, assuming an interest in the piece of music the band was playing, and Neil frowned a moment before turning towards the steps.

'I'll get changed while you make up your mind,' he declared shortly, striding off across the sand, and Jordan watched him go with some misgivings. He probably thought she was being deliberately awkward, she thought, but the idea of being one of the crowd did not appeal right now.

'My dance, I think.'

The two hands gripping her waist from behind needed no identification, and she turned towards Rhys with undisguised resentment. 'Can't you leave me alone?' she exclaimed, in a low angry voice, but when he drew her resisting body towards him, she felt a treacherous warmth invade her lower limbs.

'I should, I know,' he averred, but the compliance in his tone was not matched by the possession in his hands as he pulled her against him. 'Unfortunately, as you remarked earlier, the amount of alcohol I've consumed has somewhat weakened my resistance to your not inconsiderable charms, and in spite of your ingratitude, I'm prepared to overlook your faults—for this evening, at least.'

CHAPTER ELEVEN

Jordan gasped in indignation, but already people had noticed them together, and to fight with Rhys now, in so public a place, could only cause the kind of gossip she had wanted to avoid. And she had to go on living here, after he had returned to his home in England or Florida or wherever it was he spent most time . . .

'I don't want to dance with you,' she insisted, in an unsteady tone, and he acknowledged her protest.

'But you will,' he replied, nodding towards the hired musicians, and immediately the music changed to a languid calypso, much different from the upbeat rhythms they had been playing previously.

'Did you bribe the band?' she exclaimed, submitting to his arms about her waist, but keeping her own hands firmly between them.

'I didn't have to,' he assured her, overcoming her attempt to keep some distance between them, and allowing her to feel the muscled strength of his legs as they moved. 'I was talking to them earlier. They admired my taste.'

Jordan gasped. 'You're so sure of yourself, aren't you?'

'Not sure at all,' he retorted huskily, and his simple admission accomplished what his confidence had not.

There were few other couples dancing at this time, and Jordan guessed Lucy and Martina, and Neil, too, had all observed their participation. It didn't help her self-confidence to know that deep down her objections had been tempered by a secret excitement at the knowledge that Rhys still found her attractive, and the feel of his body touching hers was a purely sensual experience.

'Do you get the feeling we're being watched?' he asked suddenly, and her fingers curled against his shirt.

'Does that surprise you?' she murmured. 'No one expected us to speak to one another, let alone dance together.'

'I suppose you're right.' Rhys's lips brushed her hair. 'So let's really give them something to talk about, hmm?'

'What?' Jordan was apprehensive.

'Walk with me,' he said, stopping in the middle of the dance and looking down at her. 'Just along the beach.' He paused. 'Away from all these prying eyes.'

She moved her head uneasily from side to side. 'I can't.'

'Why not?' His voice was harsh now.

'Neil——'

'Ferris is in the water,' said Rhys flatly. 'He passed us a few minutes ago, wearing a pair of white trunks. I guess he didn't expect you to join him.'

Jordan looked anxiously towards the circle of figures bobbing about in the shallows. 'Are—you sure?'

'I won't forget Ferris's face,' retorted Rhys shortly. 'Come on, Jordan. Is it so much to ask? I want to talk to you about Lucy, and I can't do that here.'

'Lucy?' she queried.

Jordan looked up at him doubtfully, and Rhys took the opportunity to turn her about and propel her gently but firmly off the improvised dance floor. 'Among other things,' he agreed huskily, guiding her away from the torchlit area around the buffet tables. 'Isn't this better?' he added, as the softer light of the moon fell around them.

Jordan admitted silently that it was, but she also

acknowledged that their behaviour would not go unremarked. Nevertheless, it was a little late now to start worrying about it, and giving herself up to the demands of the moment, she fell into step beside him, when Rhys started to walk along the sand.

'You said you wanted to talk about Lucy,' she reminded him after a few moments, and he turned his head to look at her.

'Do you know why I came back to the island?' he asked, ignoring her opening, and Jordan expelled her breath carefully as she considered her reply.

'I—I assumed you wanted to check that the house was still in order. To—show it to Lucy, perhaps.'

'That's what you thought?'

'Yes.' She lifted her shoulders. 'What else is there?'

Rhys hesitated. 'You.'

'Me?' Jordan was glad of the moonlight to hide her heated skin. 'Well——' she endeavoured to keep her tone light, 'I never would have guessed!'

'Don't be facetious,' said Rhys harshly. 'It doesn't suit you.'

'Well, I'm sorry.' Jordan twisted her trembling fingers behind her. 'But you have to admit, that's an original opening, when every time you see me you blow a fuse!'

'Whose fault is that?' Rhys halted now, and she was forced to halt, too, suddenly aware of how far they had come from the reassuring lights of the party.

Jordan drew an unsteady breath. 'Are you saying it's mine?'

Rhys nodded. 'You can hardly blame me.'

'Can't I?' Jordan held up her head. 'Not even though you ordered me off your land the first time we met?'

'Oh——' Rhys pushed impatient fingers through his hair, 'I thought I'd explained that. God, I came to apologise, didn't I? Even though you wouldn't listen to me.'

Jordan bent her head, trying to calm the pounding in her chest. 'All right,' she said. 'Perhaps I was— suspicious of your motives.'

'Suspicious!' Rhys massaged the muscles at his nape. 'You were downright bloody-minded! I wanted to wring your neck!'

Jordan's lips twitched. 'I apologised, too,' she reminded him, suddenly seeing the humour in their argument. 'So—let's agree to disagree on this point. Why have you brought me here?'

Rhys looked down at her. 'Because I wanted to be alone with you.'

'But you said——'

'About Lucy, I know.' He sighed. 'Does there have to be a reason?' He turned, thrusting his hands into his pockets and gazing broodingly towards the water. 'Let's swim.'

'Swim?' Jordan gazed at him. 'But—you don't have any shorts, do you?'

He looked at her. 'So what? You're not about to ravish me, are you?'

Jordan flushed. 'We can't.'

'That word is too often used in your vocabulary,' he retorted, unfastening the belt of his slacks and propelling the zip downwards. 'I guess you're wearing a bikini, so that's all that need concern you. If you're prudish, don't look until I'm in the water.'

But she did, even though all she saw was the muscled length of his spine above the taut curve of his buttocks as he plunged into the sea. She stood for several minutes just watching his dark head moving further and further away from the shore, then she gave in to the urge to follow him. After all, if she returned to the party without him, it was bound to cause speculation, and the lure of the water was too tempting to resist.

Shedding the smock on to the sand, she ran into the waves, shivering at the first cool surge of the water. But soon the creaming surf was like warm silk against her skin, and she swam out strongly into the fast-moving current.

'You changed your mind, I see,' remarked Rhys, appearing beside her, and Jordan's pulses quickened.

'I was hot,' she said, moving away from him, but he came after her and grasped a handful of her hair.

'Not so fast,' he taunted, using her hair to draw her towards him. 'Now, don't you wish you weren't wearing a bikini? Don't you remember how good it feels to swim in the raw?'

Jordan twisted away from him, trying to avoid contact with his powerful frame. 'You do everything in the raw, don't you?' she retorted. 'Well, I don't want to. I just want you to let me go.'

'Okay.' He released her. 'But you'll regret it. I can't imagine Neil swimming in the raw—or sleeping in the raw either.'

'You know nothing about Neil,' she exclaimed, keeping a safe distance between them. 'He's everything you're not, as it happens. He's good and decent, and dependable——'

'And boring,' Rhys finished for her contemptuously. 'Has he touched you yet? Or is he saving himself for your wedding night?'

Jordan caught her breath. 'Wouldn't you like to know!' she exclaimed unsteadily.

'Yes, I would, actually,' Rhys replied, and, disturbed by his sudden movement towards her, Jordan turned and swam strongly for the shallows.

She was on the beach when he caught up with her, trying to find the right way to put on the smock, but when his hands closed on her arms, it fell from her trembling grasp.

'Oh, Jordan,' he breathed, drawing her back against him, and she felt his taut arousal unashamedly between them.

'Rhys——' she began, turning her head from side to side, but his hands had already disposed of the bootlace straps on the bikini bra, and when her breasts spilled into his hands, she was lost.

'Don't say it,' he implored, turning her to face him. 'Don't tell me I can't do this, because I must!' and his mouth found hers with unerring accuracy.

She wanted to resist him. She wanted to remember all the bad things he had done to her, and the weeks and months and years she had spent despising him and all he stood for—but she couldn't. When he coaxed her lips ever wider so that the melding of their mouths became a passionate consummation, she could only wind her arms about him, and even the skimpy bikini briefs became an intolerable barrier between them.

'God, I've wanted this,' he groaned, his hands on her hips probing the shred of fabric that divided them, and a flood of heat surged down her legs as she strained towards him.

With infinite ease, he drew her down on to the sand, and the coral grains at her back were an intoxicating reminder of their whereabouts. There was something intensely exciting about making love on the beach, and Rhys's leg imprisoning both of hers was achingly familiar.

'Touch me,' he urged huskily, and her hands explored his taut body with increasing recognition. She found she remembered every sinew, every muscle, every male angle, and his uncontrolled responses evoked a similar need inside her.

'You're beautiful!' he muttered, his mouth blazing a

trail from her throat to her breast, capturing one swollen nipple between his lips and allowing his tongue to inflame its already sensitised crest. 'And you always did taste so good . . .'

His hand stroking the inner curve of her thigh was incredibly sensuous, and when his knee nudged her legs apart, she felt the air cool against her bare flesh.

'Can we?' she whispered unsteadily, and his twisted smile was full of irony.

'How can we not?' he responded, covering her body with his, and she felt his pulsating maleness rigid against her.

'Oh, yes—yes,' she panted, unable to deny him any longer, and Rhys's mouth possessed hers as he thrust himself upon her.

The involuntary cry she uttered was stifled by his lips. And in any case, the enormous satisfaction she was experiencing more than compensated for any momentary discomfort she had had. Ten years was such a long time, she thought achingly, before the intense pleasure his sensuous movements was creating drove all other considerations from her mind. Her senses swam beneath the hungry onslaught of his mouth, and beneath her hands his skin was smooth and still damp from his swim. Her nails curled into his taut flesh as the need for fulfilment built inside her. She wanted him, she wanted *all* of him, she knew fiercely, and the little cries she was uttering gave way to gasps of ecstasy as she reached the mountain peak and felt the wild explosion . . .

The sound of voices, albeit from a distance, brought Jordan back to reality, and she turned her head anxiously towards them. She couldn't actually see anyone yet, but within minutes whoever it was would be upon them, and panic flared at the realisation of what they would find.

'Rhys!' she exclaimed frantically, trying to wriggle out from beneath him But he was still drowsy and satiated with their lovemaking, and when she endeavoured to escape, he captured her face between his hands and covered her lips with his.

'I don't want to move,' he muttered, his mouth caressing hers. 'I want to stay here all night.'

'Well, we can't.'

'Why can't we?'

'Someone's coming,' protested Jordan agitatedly. 'Come on, Rhys. We have to get dressed. Or do you want to be seen like this?'

'I don't mind,' he retorted broodingly, and Jordan drew a trembling breath.

'Well, I do!'

He rested his hands on the sand for a moment, looking down at her, and then, without another word, he rolled on to his back. 'Okay,' he said harshly, resting one arm across his forehead. 'Don't let me stop you. If your public image means that much to you, go!'

'Oh, Rhys!' Jordan scrambled to her feet and tugged on the bikini briefs he had taken from her earlier. 'Rhys—please! Put your clothes on. It could be anyone.' She paused. 'Even Lucy.'

'Why should you care about Lucy?' he demanded roughly. 'I'd have thought this was the ideal way to get your own back. Proving how—*weak* I am where you are concerned.'

'Weak?'

'Yes, weak,' he retorted grimly, at last getting to his feet. 'I came to the island to get you out of my system, Jordan, and what happens? Within a month of getting here, I'm lusting after you like some callow teenager!'

He shook his head, reaching for his pants. 'God, I must be out of my mind!'

'Rhys——'

'Forget it!' He hauled up his zip and fastened his belt. Then he pulled his sweat-shirt over his head and faced her. 'Are you ready? Then let's go and show our faces, shall we?'

They encountered the owners of the voices Jordan had overheard some way back along the beach. It was Martina and a young man Jordan didn't recognise, but she thought how typical it was that it should be the other girl who had provided the intrusion. She had probably observed their departure, Jordan reflected tensely, resentful of the piercing scrutiny they were being subjected to. It was an actual physical effort not to check on her appearance beneath the cold appraisal, and the awareness of Rhys's anger towards her didn't help.

'So there you are,' Martina remarked unnecessarily. 'We thought you must have got lost.'

'I doubt that somehow,' Rhys responded curtly. 'However, here we are, safe and sound. As you can see.'

Martina's lips tightened. 'What have you been doing, Jordan? Your hair's wet—and there's sand in it.'

'We've been swimming, and I guess the wind is stronger than we thought,' said Rhys, before Jordan could think of a response. It was true, she had not been able to get all the sand out of her hair, but now Rhys slipped his hand beneath her elbow and propelled her forward without waiting for Martina's comments.

'I—thanks,' Jordan murmured, as soon as they were out of earshot, and Rhys released her.

'Don't thank me,' he retorted. 'I don't want Martina

suggesting to Lucy that her father can't be trusted!' and reaching the circle of torches, he walked away. Jordan was left with the disturbing image of him striding grimly across to the group of young people surrounding his daughter, and a sense of desolation swept over her.

'Jordan! So there you are. Where the hell have you been? I've been looking for you.'

It was so very hard to adopt an air of composure when the man who had brought her to the party appeared beside her, but Jordan knew she owed it to Rhys to behave equally casually. 'I—went for a walk,' she admitted, avoiding Neil's eyes. 'Are you having a good time?'

'You went for a swim, too,' he accused, touching her damp hair. 'Who with? Or shall I guess?'

'I was with Rhys, I admit it,' she responded quickly, amazed at her own audacity. 'What's wrong with that? You've been with Joanna Chesney, haven't you?'

It was a pure guess, but to her astonishment, Neil went red. 'Well,' he blustered hotly, 'we are old friends. And there wasn't any harm in it.'

'Oh, Neil!' Suddenly Jordan felt intensely weary. 'I would like to go home now. Do you mind? If you do, I can always ring Karen and ask her to come and fetch me.'

'Of course not!' Neil was affronted. 'I'll take you home. But I don't think you should get upset over my friendship with Joanna. We're like brother and sister. Honestly, it's quite innocent.'

'I believe you.' Jordan pushed her hand under the weight of her hair and lifted it tiredly off her neck. If only she could say the same about her relationship with Rhys, she thought defeatedly. But no matter how she tried to fool herself, he was, and had always been, the only man she ever wanted.

CHAPTER TWELVE

THREE days later Jordan learned that Rhys and Lucy had left the island.

She had been living in a kind of daze, doing her work automatically and trying not to think about what had happened the night of the Hammonds' party. But when Karen brought the news, it was a nerve-wrenching shock, and she couldn't prevent the colour draining from her cheeks.

As luck would have it, she was alone in the office when Karen came to find her, but her sister noticed her pallor immediately. 'Hey, are you all right?' she exclaimed anxiously, coming round the desk to lay a cool hand on Jordan's temple. 'You feel hot, but your face is as white as a sheet. Don't you feel well?'

'I'm—fine,' protested Jordan hollowly, brushing Karen's hand away and endeavouring to concentrate on the invoices in front of her. 'Did—er—did we get those melons I ordered? I've got an invoice here, but no delivery note.'

'Forget about the melons.' Karen perched on the corner of Jordan's desk and refused to be dislodged. 'It's Rhys Williams again, isn't it? Heavens, I should have guessed. Barging in here, announcing blithely that he'd left without even saying goodbye. I should be hanged! I'm sorry.'

'I don't know what you mean.' Jordan rubbed her nose with a determined finger. 'Why should you imagine Rhys Williams' departure means anything to me? I've told you before. That affair is over. And as for not saying goodbye—why should he?'

'Because it would have been the decent thing to do,' declared Karen staunchly. 'I thought—after what Neil said——'

'Neil?' Jordan looked up then, unable to hide her consternation. 'What did Neil say?' She moistened her lips. 'When were you talking to him?'

Karen shrugged. 'Two days ago. You remember, he came to take you riding, but you were too busy. Or so you said.'

'Oh—then.'

'Yes, then.' Karen folded her arms. 'He was pretty annoyed, or I don't suppose he'd have said anything.'

'Well, what did he say?' exclaimed Jordan, her nerves fraying, and Karen gave her a considering look.

'He said you'd been with Rhys the night of the party.'

'Did he?' Jordan's voice was tight.

'Yes.' Karen hesitated. 'I didn't take sides, if that's what you're thinking. I mean, you're with lots of people at a party, aren't you?' She paused, then added ruefully: 'He was probably jealous.'

'Yes.' Jordan caught her lower lip between her teeth.

'And that's all he said, honestly.' Karen sighed. 'I didn't pry. Even though I'd have liked to,' she finished candidly.

Jordan shook her head. 'I suppose it's all over the island by now.'

'What? Your talking to Rhys at the party?'

'We didn't just—talk,' said Jordan wearily. 'We—oh, we left the party and went swimming together. You might as well hear it from me. Martina is unlikely to forget about it.'

'She went, too?' Karen looked perplexed.

'No.' Jordan bent her head. 'She saw us coming back. My hair was wet, and—well, she wasn't pleased that Rhys had abandoned the party.'

'And her,' said Karen fervently.

'I doubt that.' Jordan tried to be fair. 'I don't think she was ever that closely involved with him.'

'But she'd have liked to be?'

'I don't know.' Karen's persistent questions were beginning to give Jordan a headache. 'As I say, the fact that Rhys and I spent any time together is bound to be food for gossip.' She paused, and then continued determinedly: 'I don't blame him for leaving. I wish I could.'

'With Rhys?'

'Oh, Karen!' Jordan looked up at her sister helplessly. 'Stop trying to put words into my mouth. How many more times? Rhys and I mean nothing to one another. Now will you stop catechising me?'

Of course, that was not the end of it so far as Jordan was concerned. There was gossip about the island. She knew from her own staff, after walking into the middle of an argument in the kitchen that was silenced by her appearance. Even Raoul regarded her with something akin to sympathy in his dark eyes, and he was especially co-operative whenever she asked for his help.

For her own part, the nights were the worst. During the day, she succeeded in coping with her emotions, even in the face of so many well-meaning—if unwanted—acts of kindness. She was able to concentrate on managing the hotel, to the exclusion of all else, working from morning till night with a resolution that bordered on drudgery.

But at night, her feelings caught up with her. No matter how hard she had worked during the day, she still found it difficult to sleep, and dark circles appeared around her eyes. Even make-up could not entirely disguise them, and when Karen found her in the storeroom one morning, feeling dizzy with the heat, she finally lost her temper.

'That's it!' she exclaimed, grasping Jordan's arm, and marching her out into the shade of a sprawling casuarina. 'You're going to kill yourself if this goes on. Now, I forbid you to do anything else today, do you hear me? You're to rest this afternoon, and if you're no better tomorrow, I'm going to ask Doctor Chesney to come and see you.'

'Oh, Karen——'

'Don't "oh, Karen" me!' The younger girl's face was flushed with anxiety. 'Oh, I know I can't make you do anything you don't want to do, but for goodness' sake, take a look at yourself!'

Jordan sighed. 'It's very sweet of you, but——'

'It's not sweet at all. I care about you, Jordan. You're the only sister I've got. Now, please, promise me you'll do as I say. I don't want you to have a nervous breakdown, but you will if you don't let up.'

Jordan ran a weary hand over her brow. 'Perhaps you're right. Perhaps I have been trying to do too much.' She gave Karen an affectionate smile. 'All right, I'll take the day off. But don't expect me to stay in my room. I—well, I'd rather take the buggy for a drive.'

'So long as you take it easy,' said Karen, with more confidence. 'Go and see Nana, why don't you? You know she hasn't been well, and it's ages since you've seen her.'

Ages indeed, thought Jordan painfully, remembering the afternoon she had last visited Nana Fox only too well. That visit had precipitated her meeting with Rhys, and the memory was not one she wished to resurrect.

Nevertheless, driving back from Nana's that afternoon, she found her foot easing off the accelerator as she neared the drive of Rhys's house. It was all so familiar; the open gates, the cream-washed walls, the drooping scarlet hibiscus. She wondered if Tomas and Rosalie were still to be employed, or whether Rhys intended to sell the house this time. If not, she didn't think she could bear to go on supervising his property. Not now . . .

The sight of Tomas, trimming the bushes to one side of the drive, brought her to a decision. There was one way she could find out what Rhys intended to do, and that was by asking. Why go on tormenting herself with possibilities? Rosalie would tell her. Rosalie had always told her everything.

Tomas looked up in surprise when the sound of her footsteps attracted his attention. 'Missy Jordan!' he exclaimed warmly. Then, with some embarrassment, he added: 'If you've come to see Mr Williams, he ain't here.'

'I know that, Tomas.' Jordan forced a slight smile. 'Er—is Rosa about? I thought she might offer me a cup of tea.'

'She's in the kitchen, or noddin' in her chair outside,' Tomas declared, evidently relieved that Jordan was not to be disappointed. 'You just go on round. She'll be mighty glad to see you, I know.'

'Thanks.'

Jordan lifted her hand, and continued on round the house to where the verandah overlooked the beach. Then, mounting the steps, she followed the wooden structure round to the side of the building, where a vine-covered porch gave access to the domestic apartments.

As Tomas had predicted, Rosalie was seated on the wooden bench just outside the door, nodding over her sewing. But like her husband she had heard Jordan's approach, and her eyes widened at the sight of the girl's slim figure.

'Missy Jordan!' she exclaimed, coming to her feet. 'Tch, I didn't expect to see you. Didn't Tomas tell you——'

'——that Rhys isn't here? I already knew,' replied Jordan, waving her back on to her seat. 'Don't worry—I know he's gone back to England. It's common knowledge in Eleutha.'

'Then common knowledge ain't right,' said Rosalie, sinking back on to her seat and folding her hands. 'Mr Williams isn' in England, he's in Nc.. York. Had a message from that manager of his, Mr Withers, askin' him if he'd do a concert in aid of some relief organisation, or somethin'. He didn' refuse.'

'I see.' Jordan moistened her dry lips. 'So——he's coming back.'

'I don' think so.' Rosalie shrugged. 'He only planned on stayin' here a month, you know, and that time's almost up. I guess he's got other commitments after New York.'

'Oh.' Jordan knew Rosalie's answer shouldn't have depressed her, but it did. Just for a second, she had half believed he was coming back to the island, and while that news need not have meant anything, there was always the possibility that it might.

'You feelin' the heat?' Rosalie was looking at her strangely, and Jordan struggled to pull herself together.

'A—a bit,' she confessed, running her damp palms down the seams of her cotton pants. 'It is humid, isn't it? Do you think it's going to rain?'

Rosalie shrugged. Then, choosing her words with care, she said, astonishingly; 'Why d'you let him go?'

Jordan caught her breath. 'I beg your pardon?'

'I said—why d'you let him go?' said Rosalie succinctly. 'Seems like I got the impression that you used to care somethin' about him. That mornin' when you came here, I was sure you were gettin' set to put things right.'

Jordan gasped. 'Rosa!'

'Well! Young Lucy thought so, too. I heard her ask Mr Williams if he was in love with you, and he didn't deny it, as I recall.'

Jordan, who had been supporting herself against the porch, straightened. 'I think I'd better be going, Rosa,' she said, unwilling to listen to any more of the black woman's fantasising. 'I don't want to get caught if it is going to rain, and——'

'I was wrong, you know,' Rosalie interrupted her, bending her head over her sewing again. 'When his wife came here lookin' for him, I shouldn' have told you.'

'What?' Jordan stared at her. 'What are you talking about, Rosa? I was grateful to you for telling me. Good heavens, can you imagine how embarrassed I'd have been if I'd come here and found them together?'

'But you wouldn't,' insisted Rosalie stubbornly. 'If I hadn't warned you, you might never have known. Mr Williams would have sent her away, and that would have been the end of it.'

'Rosa!' Jordan was horrified. 'What are you saying? That if I hadn't known Rhys was married, that would have been all right?'

'He'd have got a divorce,' said Rosalie firmly. 'Like he intended to do all along. Like he thought he had done.'

'Do you really believe that?' Jordan despised herself for arguing with the woman, but it was better than keeping it all inside. 'Look, Rhys wasn't a child. He knew divorce papers had to be filed. If he thought Jennifer was filing them, then he should have checked, not left it to chance.'

Rosalie shook her head. 'You forget, he wasn't in England that much. Those bands, they're always goin' on tour. And he trusted that solicitor of his to do what was right. But that woman had no intention of lettin' him divorce her—not with all that money he was makin'.'

'Oh, Rosa!'

'I'm right, I know it.' Rosalie nodded her head. 'Lived with that for ten years, I have. Then, when Mr Williams came back, I thought everythin' was goin' to be all right.'

'Well, you were wrong.' Jordan put an unsteady hand up to the formal coil of hair at her nape. 'And besides, there was Lucy to consider. You can't deny Rhys's responsibility there.'

'He did,' remarked Rosalie sagely, and Jordan sighed.

'Then why is she living with him now?'

'Her mother was killed.'

'So?'

'They didn't leave here together, you know, Mr Williams and his wife. Even after you had that row with him, he still threw her and the child out.'

'I know.'

Jordan felt the prick of tears behind her eyes. Oh, she knew that all right, she thought bitterly. After her first sense of outrage had been appeased, she had actually considered going after him, to beg him to forgive her for disbelieving him when he said Lucy was not his child. But then her father had had his accident, and by the time he was well enough for her to leave him, Jennifer had been dead and buried and the papers had been full of stories of Rhys and his motherless little daughter.

'Anyway, I think you're a fool,' said Rosalie, with a sniff. 'You're in love with him, anyone can see that.

Comin' here all those years, carin' for his property like
it was your own. Ain' no sense in it, less'n you intend
to do somethin' about it.'

'What can I do about it?' Jordan wrapped her arms
around herself. 'It's been too long.'

'You don't believe that, any more than he does,'
retorted Rosalie sharply. 'And what can he do? You
rejected him, not the other way around.'

Jordan quivered. 'You're an old romantic, Rosa.
Life's not like that.'

'Isn' it? So what's eatin' you?'

'What do you mean?'

'I mean you're as skinny as a lath, and you've got
them black rings around your eyes. What you got to
lose, girl? Tell him how you feel, and see what he
says.'

'How can I?' Jordan was amazed that she was
actually considering it. 'Rosa——'

'Get on the next plane to New York. I know where
he's stayin'. Take a chance. Isn't life worth it?'

'You're crazy, Rosa!'

'I ain't crazy. You are, if you don't believe that
man still cares about you.'

'You don't understand, Rosa——'

'What don' I understand?'

'Oh——' Jordan spread her hands, unable to tell her
about the Hammonds' party, and the way it had
ended, 'there's so much you don't know.'

'I know Mr Williams was like a bear with a sore
head the day after that party he went to,' Rosalie
declared, as if reading Jordan's thoughts. 'And I know
how many nights he was down here, traipsin' round
the house when he ought to have been gettin' his
sleep. And the alcohol he drank!' She lifted her hands
in resignation. 'You should have been here to see it.
I'm not lyin'. Mr Williams is not a happy man.'

Jordan shook her head. 'I can't go to New York.'

'Why not?'

'Because I can't.'

'That's no answer.'

'I've got the hotel to run,' protested Jordan weakly. 'And what if he refused to see me?'

'You think he would?'

Jordan bent her head. 'I don't know.'

'At least try.' Rosalie got to her feet and went indoors, only to emerge seconds later with a scrap of paper. 'Here's his address. It's an apartment building, or so he said. It belongs to a friend of his who's out of town.'

Jordan shook her head again. 'Look, Rosa, I know you mean well, but it's no use you giving that to me. I—I can't go to New York. I just can't.'

Jordan was still silently protesting the sanity of what she was doing when the Eastern Airlines jet landed in New York. It was Karen who had booked the flight, Karen who had bought her tickets, and Karen who had contacted the hotel of a family friend in the city and arranged for her sister to stay overnight there.

Jordan hadn't intended to tell Karen of her conversation with Rosalie. When she drove back to the hotel on the island, she had determined not to mention the fact that she had called at the house at Planter's Point, but it hadn't turned out that way. She was in her room, drying her hair after a shower, when Karen came to find her, and the younger girl's casual enquiry as to whether she had seen either of the Simms,' when she passed the house had brought a wave of betraying colour to her cheeks.

Of course, she couldn't lie about it, but she was not to know how revealing her unwilling answers had been. In no time at all, Karen had solicited the information that Rhys was not in England, but New York, and without really wanting to, Jordan found herself voicing the doubts that Rosalie's words had aroused.

'You mean—she doesn't think Lucy is Rhys's child?' Karen exclaimed incredulously, perching on the end of the bed.

'I said she had doubts,' amended Jordan, wishing she hadn't started this. 'Oh, you know what Rosa's like. She knew why I'd gone there. She just wanted to—cheer me up, I suppose.'

'Why did you go there?' asked Karen pointedly. 'You told me that affair was over, but it's not, is it? Not as far as you're concerned anyway.'

'Oh, Karen . . .'

'There you go again, treating me like a child! I'm not a child, Jordan. I'm nearly twenty-one. I do understand the facts of life. Why can't you trust me? I can be trusted, you know.'

'I know, I know.' Jordan leant across and squeezed Karen's hand. 'It's just—well, it's not easy for me to talk about it.'

Karen hesitated. 'But you are still in love with Rhys, aren't you? And whether Lucy is or is not his daughter doesn't really matter any more.'

Jordan bent her head. 'It should.'

'But it doesn't.'

'I suppose not.' Jordan sighed. 'Does that sound terrible to you?'

'It sounds like the truth,' averred Karen drily. 'For heaven's sake, how long have you known?'

Jordan shook her head. 'I don't know. Since Rhys came back to the island, I suppose. As—as soon as I saw him——'

'—at the hotel——'

'No, not at the hotel.' Jordan hesitated a moment

and then briefly described their confrontation on the beach. 'He looked just the same,' she said unsteadily. 'I couldn't believe it.'

'So that was why you wore those ghastly clothes when he and Lucy came to the hotel,' exclaimed Karen nodding. 'Poor Rhys! And he came to apologise, didn't he? I thought it was odd at the time, but you wouldn't talk about it. I assumed it was to do with something he'd done before he went away.'

Jordan picked up her brush and ran her palm over the bristles. 'He said he wanted us to start over. Oh, not emotionally,' she added, flushing. 'Just to be civil with one another. Only I was so uptight I wouldn't talk to him. That was why I went to the house.'

'You went to—*his* house?' Karen stared at her.

'Yes. The next day.' Jordan's colour came and went. 'Don't ask me why. I just—had to see him again.'

'To apologise, I suppose,' remarked Karen with some humour. 'Oh, Jordan! And you pretended you didn't care!'

Jordan shrugged. 'I didn't want you to feel sorry for me.'

'Why not?'

'I can't bear sympathy. I had all I could take when—when Rhys went away. Everyone was so—so sympathetic, I just wanted to die.'

'But you didn't.'

'No.' Jordan sniffed. 'People don't, do they? And—well, Daddy had his accident, didn't he? What is it they say about ill winds?'

Karen frowned. 'And you never forgave him? Rhys, I mean.'

'I——' Jordan hesitated. 'I—yes, I thought about it. And if—if Daddy hadn't been taken ill, I had actually considered going to see Rhys, to tell him I believed him about—about the child.'

'So what stopped you?'

'By the time Daddy was recovering, Rhys's wife had been killed in that plane crash. When I read about him—looking after Lucy, I assumed he'd been lying all along.'

Karen blinked. 'Do you still believe that?'

'I don't know.' Jordan hunched her shoulders. 'What do you think?'

'I think the way you feel about each other is more important than who was right and who was wrong,' said Karen evenly. 'What does Rosa say? Does she think Rhys still cares about you?'

'I can't take Rosa's word for anything,' Jordan protested. 'Oh, she says he's not happy, that he drinks a lot, and that the day after Cilla Hammonds' party he was bad-tempered, but what does that mean? He may be having problems with his work.'

'With more than a dozen platinum discs behind him, and his current album selling all over the world, what do you think?' Karen grimaced. 'Come on, Jordan! You know better than that.'

'Do I?'

Karen groaned. 'You must have some reason to feel the way you do. Are you telling me you and Rhys just *talked* that night at the party?'

'Well—no, but——'

'But nothing.' Karen pushed herself up from the bed. 'If I were you, I'd go and see him; tell him how you feel. Or are you going to wait another ten years before you come to your senses?'

CHAPTER THIRTEEN

IT was early evening by the time the taxi dropped Jordan at the entrance to the exclusive block of apartments overlooking Madison Avenue. She hadn't consciously been delaying the moment when she must come here, but driving in from Kennedy Airport at the start of the rush-hour, and checking in to her hotel, had all taken time. In addition the Lorrimers, who owned the hotel where she was staying, had insisted on her taking tea with them and asking lots of questions about herself and Karen and Trade Winds, and by the time Jordan left Third Avenue it was after seven o'clock.

Even so, it had taken a great deal of nerve to pluck up the courage to make the short journey across town. The nearer she came to meeting Rhys again the more uncertain she felt, and the small store of confidence which had helped her to board the plane in Miami had long since been dissipated. It now seemed the height of conceit to imagine that Rhys might be pleased to see her, and the idea that he might enjoy humiliating her again could not be dislodged. She shouldn't have come, she told herself fiercely, as she stood shivering on the pavement. October in New York was not like October in the islands, and in spite of the thickness of her hooded coat, the wind struck chillingly into her bones.

'Want something, lady?'

The insinuating voice close to her ear made her start, and she swung round in some alarm to find a flashily-dressed individual regarding her with unconcealed admiration. 'You need any help, lady?' he added, his familiarity indicative of the kind of help he thought she needed, and shocked into sudden action, Jordan scurried through the swing glass doors into the apartment building.

As she glanced back over her shoulder, half afraid that the man who had attempted to solicit her might be following, another hand touched her sleeve, and she jerked back in alarm from the uniformed commissionaire who had accosted her.

'I—what do you want?'

'I didn't mean to frighten you, miss.'

The commissionaire released her sleeve, but he was nevertheless regarding her with some suspicion, and belatedly Jordan guessed he was probably employed to check on everyone who entered the building. Perhaps he had witnessed her encounter with the tout, she speculated anxiously. Perhaps he even suspected she knew him. It seemed imperative to explain that she had not been encouraging the man's attentions, and forcing a smile to her lips, she said: 'I'm not used to being approached like that. I don't live in the city, you see.'

'No, miss.' The man was noncommittal.

'No.' Jordan took a deep breath. 'I—er—I've come to visit someone who—who's staying here. Apartment 43B. Is it all right if I take the lift?'

'The person you've come to see would be—who, miss?'

Jordan looked longingly at the bank of lifts. Then she sighed. 'It's a Mr Williams,' she said awkwardly. 'Mr Rhys Williams. He's staying here for a few days in—in the apartment of a friend.'

'And that friend would be?'

Jordan looked blank. 'I don't know.'

'You don't know the name of the person your— friend is staying with?'

'He's not staying with anyone.' Jordan coloured. 'I thought I explained. He's just—borrowing the apartment. Surely you must know that.'

The man shrugged. 'Maybe.'

'Well, this is the address, isn't it?' Jordan produced the scrap of paper Rosalie had given her, realising too late how grubby it had become. Anyone could write an address on a piece of paper. It didn't prove anything at all.

The man examined the paper and then handed it back to her. 'That's apartment 43B, okay,' he agreed flatly. 'But no one said anything to me about— about——?'

'Jordan Lucas.' She sighed. 'Rhys is staying here, then?'

'Could be.'

'So couldn't I just go up? I'm quite trustworthy, honestly.'

'Couldn't do that, miss. Not without confirmation. But I will ring Mr Williams and tell him you're here. If he wants to see you, then okay.'

Jordan's shoulders sagged. 'Oh, if you must,' she muttered wearily, preparing herself for the worst, and the commissionaire crossed to his desk and picked up the telephone.

She tried not to listen to the one-sided conversation, but even so, it soon became apparent that there was a problem. It didn't surprise her at all when the commissionaire put down the receiver and shook his head, and she had started for the door when he said sharply: 'Wait!'

'What for?' Jordan turned. 'He doesn't want to see me, does he?' She paused. 'Oh, you couldn't call a taxi for me, could you? I—well, I'd rather not hang about outside.'

The commissionaire pushed the phone back on to

the desk and came towards her. 'Mr Williams isn't there,' he said flatly. 'But someone's coming down to see you. You shouldn't jump to conclusions. It's not a good idea.'

Jordan frowned. 'Someone's coming down to see me?' she echoed. 'Who? Lucy?'

'Lucy? Oh, you mean Miss Williams,' said the commissionaire drily. 'No, it's not her. It's someone else. Mr Williams' manager.'

'Mr Withers?' Jordan had never met the man, but she had heard of him, and apparently deciding he could trust her after all, the commissionaire retired behind his desk.

'You got it,' he agreed laconically, subsiding into his chair. 'Take a seat.' He indicated the armchairs in the waiting area. 'He won't be long.'

Jordan didn't sit down. She was too tensed up for that, and when a burly little man emerged from the nearest elevator, she looked at him anxiously.

'Miss Lucas?' he asked, coming towards her, and Jordan nodded. 'Rhys didn't tell me you were coming, but am I glad to see you!'

Jordan rescued her hand from his enthusiastic grasp and gazed at him worriedly. 'Is something wrong? The commissionaire said Rhys isn't here. Is he at the theatre?'

'The theatre?' Bernie Withers blinked for a moment, and then, as if realising what she meant, he shook his head. 'No, no, he's at the hospital,' he exclaimed impatiently. 'I'll take you there now. I guess you'd like to see him.'

Jordan swayed. 'Rhys is in hospital?' she gasped weakly.

'Rhys? Hell no, it's Lucy. Didn't he tell you?' The little man shook his head. 'She was knocked down by a crazy motorist yesterday evening. They're operating on her at this moment. She needed a transfusion, and they had some difficulty in matching the blood.'

The hospital Lucy had been taken to was some distance from the apartment building, and on the way there in the taxi, Jordan tried to explain that Rhys hadn't known she was coming to New York. But no matter what she said, Bernie seemed incapable of taking it in, and eventually Jordan gave up trying to convince him and stayed silent.

'Is—is he alone at the hospital?' she asked at last, and Bernie turned from staring out the window to look at her.

'No. No, Chas is with him,' he answered swiftly. 'I would have been there, too, but someone had to make the arrangements about postponing the concert.'

'Chas?' Jordan blinked. 'Oh—you mean one of the band.'

'Rhys's closest friend,' amended Bernie, turning back to the window. 'They've been together since the band was formed. It was lucky Chas was here.'

'Yes.' Jordan's fingers tortured the strap of her handbag. 'Is she—do you think she's going to be all right?'

'Lucy?' Bernie shrugged. 'I hope so. Rhys thinks the world of her.'

'Yes.'

Jordan acknowledged his statement with an unwelcome sense of loss. Lucy was Rhys's daughter, after all. How could she have ever doubted it?

The huge teaching hospital was a bustling hive of activity. The accident and emergency sections were already in demand, even at this early hour of the evening, and ambulances whined past them as the taxi let them out at the reception area.

Inside, the bright lights were dazzling, but Bernie

led the way confidently to where two nurses were stationed behind a semi-circular desk. 'Is it okay if we go up to the twenty-third floor?' he enquired, his cockney accent sounding strange in these surroundings, and the younger nurse took his name before checking it with her superior.

'That's okay,' the elder of the two nurses said after a moment. 'You were here with Mr Williams earlier, weren't you? You can go up to the waiting area. Miss Williams is still in surgery.'

'Thanks.'

Bernie patted the desk in gratitude, and then he and Jordan walked down a cork-tiled corridor to where a bank of lifts was situated. The massive lift that transported them up to the twenty-third floor was big enough to take two stretchers, and Jordan's nerves tightened as they emerged into what looked like another reception area. But although her eyes darted anxiously over the few people present, there was no one who even faintly resembled Rhys, and she sucked in her breath a little tremulously at this second anti-climax.

Bernie knew the way, however, and Jordan had to quicken her step to keep pace with him as he passed through swinging fire doors and turned down yet another corridor. But at the end of the corridor was another waiting area, and Jordan was still some distance away when she recognised Rhys. He was sitting on the edge of one of the tubular, leather-seated armchairs provided for waiting relatives, his arms resting along his thighs, his head bent in weary anticipation. She guessed it was Chas Pepper seated at the other side of him. He, unlike Rhys, was leaning back in his chair and gazing broodingly at the ceiling. But both men gave the appearance of long-controlled impatience, and Jordan felt instinctively that she was an intruder.

'I—perhaps I ought to wait at the hotel,' she whispered, catching Bernie's sleeve, and he turned to look at her in surprise.

'Wait at the hotel?' he echoed, speaking in his normal voice, and immediately two pairs of eyes turned in their direction.

Jordan saw Rhys's face mirror his sense of disbelief that she should be here, and she could hardly continue to put one foot in front of the other as he rose unsteadily to his feet. He stood there, swaying a little, staring at her, and then his attention switched to Bernie and his voice came out harsh and unforgiving: 'Why the hell did you tell *her*?'

'I didn't!' As Jordan came to a shuddering stop, Bernie made a defensive gesture. 'I thought you'd told her yourself.' He turned to look blankly at her. 'Why didn't you tell me Rhys didn't know were here?'

Jordan's face went white, and then red, and then white again. 'I did,' she got out tremulously. 'In the taxi. But you weren't listening to me.'

'Now look here——'

'Hey, cool it, you lot!' With Bernie starting to bluster, and Rhys standing cold and forbidding, as if he was carved from stone, Chas Pepper came lazily out of his chair. 'Does it matter how she got here? She's here. Hi, Jordan. It's been a long time.'

'I'd better go.' In spite of Chas's efforts to defuse the situation, Jordan knew she couldn't take any more of this. 'I—I hope Lucy's okay. Give her my regards!' and without waiting for any response, she turned and hurried back along the corridor.

Rhys caught her before she reached the fire doors. His hand grasped her sleeve, spinning her round to face him, and the force of his action sent her thudding back against the sound-proofed wall. Her head hit the panelling with a sickening crack, and she gazed at him a little dazedly as he imprisoned her there between his hands.

'If I hurt you, I'm sorry,' he said harshly, though his expression was anything but apologetic. 'I just want to know what you're doing here. If Bernie didn't send for you, was it Chas?'

Jordan struggled to regain her breath. 'No one— sent for me,' she got out jerkily. 'I didn't know about Lucy's accident until I got here. How—how is she, by the way? Mr Withers told me she'd had a transfusion.'

Rhys studied her pale face without replying for several unnerving seconds, then his eyes darkened. 'If you didn't know about Lucy, why are you in New York? Don't tell me you've come to see the concert.'

Jordan trembled. 'You haven't told me about Lucy,' she reminded him evasively. 'Mr Withers told me there was an accident. How badly was she hurt?'

'I'll get to Lucy in a minute,' said Rhys harshly, his eyes glittering with suppressed emotion. 'Jordan, answer me, damn you! What are you doing here?'

Jordan concentrated on a point just above the unbuttoned collar of his shirt and tried to ignore the disturbing glimpse of fine dark hair that grew there. 'I —I came to—to see you,' she admitted scarcely audibly. 'I—I wanted to speak to you——'

'You're speaking to me now,' he told her, glancing round impatiently when a nurse passed by them and gave them a curious look. 'Get to the point, why don't you?'

'I—I can't talk here,' said Jordan unhappily. 'Maybe later . . .'

'Now,' he insisted roughly. 'What's the matter? Did Ferris find out about us? Is he coming looking for me with a gun?'

There was sarcasm in his voice, but there was something else, too, something that wrung her heart.

And in spite of the anguish his words might have provoked, Jordan ignored his bitterness.

'What could Neil find out?' she asked, facing him bravely. 'You evidently don't want me, so why should he feel the need to defend me?'

Rhys straightened abruptly, his features contorting as if she had delivered a physical slap in the face. Breathing shallowly, he met her tremulous gaze with sombre-eyed suspicion, and Jordan's confidence wavered as he continued his appraisal.

'Look, I've come at the wrong time,' she muttered unsteadily, gathering the lapels of her coat about her throat. 'I'm so sorry about Lucy. Believe me, if there's anything I can do . . .'

'There is,' said Rhys, speaking at last. 'You can stay with me. I—Chas needs a break. He's been here since last night, and he needs a rest.'

'So do you,' said Jordan impulsively, and Rhys ran a weary hand over his haggard features.

'I'm okay,' he said flatly, and then: 'Will you stay?'

'If you want me to.'

'I want you to,' he essayed, gesturing back towards the waiting area, and with a helpless little shrug, Jordan preceded him back along the corridor.

They reached the waiting area just as a man in a white overall came through glass doors to their right. 'Mr Williams?' he said, glancing from Bernie Withers to Chas Pepper, and leaving Jordan, Rhys went forward.

'I'm Rhys Williams,' he said. 'Do you have some news?'

'Ah, yes, Mr Williams.' The man nodded pleasantly. 'I should have recognised you. My name's Alexander. I'm the surgeon who operated on your daughter.'

'And?' said Rhys succinctly. 'How is she? Is she going to be all right?'

'I believe so,' the surgeon nodded, and Jordan saw the way Rhys's shoulders sagged with relief at the news. 'If you'd like to come with me, you can see her. She's still unconscious, of course, but we managed to locate the bleeding and drain the cavity, and I see no reason why she shouldn't make a complete recovery.'

'Thank God!' Rhys glanced round at Jordan, and then, as if having to force his mind to other things, he turned back to Doctor Alexander. 'I would like to see her,' he added steadily. 'And thanks. I can't tell you what this means to me.'

'It's my job,' said the surgeon simply, and after exchanging a brief handshake with Chas, Rhys followed him back through the glass doors.

It was an emotional moment, and one which Jordan felt she had no part of. But when she would have turned away, Chas slipped his hand through her arm. 'Don't go.'

'I—Rhys doesn't want me,' she protested in embarrassment. 'Not right now anyway. I—er—I'll leave you my address. He can get in touch with me tomorrow, if he wants to.'

'Tomorrow? Don't be a fool.' Chas grimaced. 'He needs you tonight, not tomorrow. My God, I thought he was going to pass out when you came down the corridor!'

Jordan looked sideways at him. 'Why?'

'Why do you think? Hell, I've just spent the last twenty-four hours with him, Jordan, and your name has hardly been off his lips.'

'*My* name?' Jordan blinked.

'Your name,' said Chas flatly. 'You must know how he feels about you. When you appeared out of nowhere, I thought he must have contacted you himself. Goodness knows, he needed you.'

'Rhys *needed* me?'

'Stop repeating everything I say.' Chas shrugged. 'From what he's been saying, I'd have thought there was no doubt about it.'

Jordan swallowed. 'Are you sure?'

'Of course I'm sure.' Chas snorted. 'That's why he blamed himself for Lucy's accident. If it hadn't been for you, he reckons he wouldn't have come to New York.'

Jordan stared at him. 'But—why?'

'Well, he was supposed to be on holiday. When Bernie rang and put the idea to him, he could have refused. But, according to Rhys, he couldn't get through to you, so he copped out.'

'Is that what he said?'

'More or less.' Chas sighed. 'What went wrong with you two? Ten years ago, you had it made!'

'Ten years ago I didn't know about Jennifer,' said Jordan quietly.

'Jennifer!' Chas was scathing.

'She was his wife.'

'She was a money-grubbing little bitch!' retorted Chas savagely. 'I know she's dead and she can't defend herself, but she made Rhys's life a misery. Luckily for him she walked out before he made the big time. He was only eighteen when they got married, you know. He'd forgotten all about her until she turned up on Eleutha.'

'She said—*Rosa* said—she'd been looking for him for ages,' said Jordan unevenly.

'I bet she had.' Chas grimaced. 'After Jack Costa gave her the elbow, she was desperate. It's not so easy to find a meal ticket with a kid hanging round your neck.'

Jordan bent her head. 'Poor Lucy!'

'Yeah!' Chas nodded. 'It's a cruel thing to say, I know, but the luckiest thing that ever happened to her was when her mother was killed. Rhys took responsibility for her, you see, and after the kind of upbringing he had had, there was no way he was going to leave Lucy to be brought up in the care of the local council.'

Jordan stared at him, hardly daring to believe her ears. 'Lucy—Lucy had no—legal rights?'

'Damn right.' Chas was vehement. 'Didn't you know Rhys took a blood test, just to prove he wasn't her father? It was the only way he could get Jennifer off his back. But then—when she was killed . . .'

Jordan quivered. 'I didn't know—about the blood test.'

'No, you wouldn't,' said Chas, drawing away from her now. 'I mean, you didn't want to know, did you? You wouldn't even talk to him. Rhys was pretty cut up about that.'

Jordan shook her head. 'I didn't think there was any point.'

'Rhys thought there was. He thought you were in love with him.'

'I was!' Jordan bit her lip. 'I *am*. Oh, you don't understand, I was too young to think sensibly. And afterwards—when Rhys took Lucy——'

'—you took the easy way out.'

'It wasn't easy!' Jordan was defensive. 'I just wasn't that sure of myself. It wasn't as if we were engaged or anything.'

'A ring means that much to you?'

'Yes. No. Oh, I don't know . . .'

Chas shrugged. 'Well, Rhys can be stubborn, too. I guess he thought he'd get over you. There's certainly been no shortage of females willing to prove his theory these past ten years.'

Jordan winced. 'And has he?'

Chas looked at her. 'What do you think?'

Jordan lifted her shoulders. 'He—hasn't.'

'You'd better believe it,' said Chas, with sudden emotion. 'Hey, Bernie——' He turned to the little man who had been trying to make himself invisible during their conversation. 'Let's go and get a beer. We're not needed here right now. Jordan's going to wait for Rhys, aren't you?'

Jordan nodded, then she touched Chas's sleeve. 'Thanks—for everything.'

'Don't thank me.' Chas pulled a wry face. 'If it hadn't been for me, Jennifer would never have split you two up in the first place. Only don't tell Rhys I told you.'

'What do you mean?' Jordan stared at him.

'It was Petra who told Jennifer where Rhys was,' explained Chas drily. 'Do you remember Petra? I always suspected she was only using me to get to Rhys. Then, when she found out about you, she decided to make some mischief.'

CHAPTER FOURTEEN

ONCE she was left alone, much of Jordan's confidence melted. It had seemed natural to accept what Chas had told her while he was there, but it was not so easy now that he and Bernie Withers had gone. The waiting room was bleak and empty, her own reasons for being there lacking in substance, and although she obtained some coffee from the automatic machine provided, even its restoring flavour could not dispel her apprehension.

Now and again, the doors leading to the surgical wards opened and a doctor or a nurse passed through, but they paid little attention to Jordan. Apart from the faint acknowledgement of a lifted eyebrow, or the tentative beginnings of a smile, they were too absorbed in their own affairs to offer her any consolation, and by the time Rhys appeared, her doubts about this mission had all been revived.

Rhys came into the waiting area wearily, pushing back his hair with a tired hand, and turning to bid farewell to the doctor who had accompanied him. 'Go home and get some rest, Mr Williams,' the surgeon advised him kindly. 'I'll ring you as soon as I have any news. Don't worry, Lucy's going to be all right.'

'Thank you.'

As Rhys shook hands with the doctor, Jordan got to her feet, and Doctor Alexander's eyes moved speculatively over to her. 'Is this—your wife, Mr Williams?' he asked, nodding politely towards her.

'No.' Rhys's mouth tightened as he made the introduction. 'Miss—Lucas is just a friend.' Then, before any further questions could be asked, he ushered Jordan across the floor. 'You have my number. I'll be waiting for your call.'

His hand dropped from her arm before they reached the fire doors, and their footsteps crunched softly over the rubber flooring. He didn't speak until they had reached the lifts and were safely inside, and even then his words were formal and detached.

'Have Chas and Bernie left?'

'Yes.' Jordan's response was somewhat breathy. 'They said they'd see you later. I—how is Lucy?'

'She'll be okay.' Rhys put a hand against the wall of the lift to support himself. 'It was a crazy thing she did—stepping off the kerb like that. You couldn't blame the motorist. He didn't stand a chance.'

'Oh, but Mr Withers said——'

'Take no notice of Bernie. He's biased,' said Rhys drily. 'It was an accident, pure and simple. If it's anyone's fault it's mine, for bringing her to New York.'

'You can't blame yourself!' Jordan sighed. 'It could have happened in London just as easily.'

Rhys looked down at the floor of the lift. 'Yes— well, perhaps you're right. Maybe I'll feel differently when I know she's better. Right now, it's easier to accept the responsibility.'

'Easier?' Jordan stared at him. 'What do you mean?'

Rhys looked up, his eyes remote. 'If I have to think about Lucy, I don't have time to think about myself. And that makes life bearable.'

Jordan was still trying to understand this when the lift stopped at the ground floor, and she accompanied him along the corridor to the reception area almost absently. She was hardly aware of the small stir Rhys's appearance caused among the nurses, and only when they emerged into the cold night air did she begin to take notice of her surroundings again.

'We'll go to the apartment,' said Rhys, leading the way to where a sleek limousine was waiting. 'That is, if you're coming back with me. I guess Rosa must have given you the telephone number and that's how you came to speak to Bernie.'

'As a matter of fact, she gave me your address,' said Jordan softly. 'I went to the apartment earlier on. That's how I learned where you were.'

Rhys unlocked the door at her side of the car and in the lights from the hospital she could see his tense expression. 'You came to New York to find me?' he demanded harshly.

'I told you that already,' Jordan answered, looking up at him, and swinging open her door, Rhys walked swiftly round the bonnet.

'Get in,' he directed, opening his own door, and Jordan's heart thumped unsteadily as he coiled his length beside her.

The ignition fired at the first attempt, and Rhys reversed the car out of its bay. The powerful Cadillac responded smoothly beneath his hands, and as they turned out of the hospital gates Rhys explained, rather stiltedly, that he had use of the car along with the apartment.

'They both belong to a friend of mine,' he said, accelerating towards the first set of traffic signals. 'What did you think of the apartment? It's a little overpowering, isn't it?'

'I didn't see the apartment,' said Jordan uncomfortably. 'The doorman—commissionaire— wouldn't let me in. Not until he'd checked with you. Only you weren't there, so Mr Withers came down. I think he thought you'd sent for me.'

'Mmm.' Rhys made a sound of acknowledgment. 'Bernie would think that. Everything's black and white to him.'

Jordan looked across at him. 'Not to you?'

'No.' Rhys concentrated on the busy road ahead of them. 'People aren't like that. They have emotions—feelings; and failings, as you'd probably agree.'

Jordan bent her head. 'Did you want me to come? Were you glad to see me?'

Rhys shook his head. 'That depends.'

She felt chilled. 'On what?'

'On why you're here.' Rhys permitted himself a brief glance in her direction. 'Are you sure Chas didn't get in touch with you?'

'Of course, I'm sure.' Jordan moistened her lips. 'But would it matter if he had?'

Rhys sighed. 'I don't know.'

Jordan's brow furrowed. 'You're not making much sense.'

'No.' His fingers slid round the wheel. 'I guess I'm tired. I've been at the hospital since last night.'

Jordan hesitated. 'Would you rather I went away again? I'm staying with some friends on Third Avenue. You could take me there, if you'd rather.'

It took a lot to make that statement, and after it was made, Jordan waited apprehensively for Rhys's reply. If he sent her away now, she would know it was over. And after what Chas had told her, how could she blame Rhys if he did?

'No!' Rhys's response was curt, but instantaneous. 'We'll go to the apartment,' he added tautly. 'I need a shower and a change of clothes. I managed to shave with one of those disposable razors in the men's room, but I need to freshen up. Then we'll talk.'

They left the car at the entrance to the underground parking area that ran beneath the apartments. Another uniformed attendant would park it, and Rhys handed him a twenty-dollar bill along with the keys.

'Thank you, Mr Williams,' the man saluted him

gratefully, and Jordan gave Rhys an amazed look as they walked into the building.

'Twenty dollars!' she exclaimed. 'Just for parking your car!'

'It's only money,' said Rhys drily, as the doorman Jordan had seen previously rose to greet them. 'Good evening, Shannon. I believe you met Miss Lucas earlier.'

Shannon grinned a little ruefully. 'Yes, sir. Hello again, Miss Lucas. You found him, after all.'

Jordan smiled. 'Yes.' She glanced awkwardly at Rhys. 'Thank you for your help.'

'My pleasure,' averred the doorman politely, and Jordan found herself entering one of the steel-lined lifts which had looked so desirable on her last visit.

Rhys leaned against the wall of the lift as it whisked them up forty-three floors in approximately as many seconds. When the doors opened on to a discreetly-lit corridor, carpeted in a finely-woven woollen broadloom, Jordan felt as if her stomach were still somewhere around the tenth floor, and her legs felt like jelly as she followed Rhys's lead.

A panelled door, lightly grained, and piped with gold, opened into a long narrow hallway. Rhys waited until she had followed him inside, before locking the door again and attaching a safety chain. Then he led the way along the hall and into the spacious living room.

As he switched on the shaded lamps, Jordan saw at once what he had meant before. The décor was almost completely white, the only real splash of colour coming from a bowl of yellow and gold chrysanthemums, set rather incongruously on a glass table in the middle of the floor. Everything else— carpet, blinds, velvet sofas, and tubular steel furniture—echoed the monotonous absence of character, and she turned on her heel to absorb the full effect.

'Ghastly, isn't it?' said Rhys, tossing his keys on to the cocktail cabinet and helping himself to a generous measure of Scotch. 'Lucy bought the flowers, just before—well, just before she had the accident. I guess the daily woman thought they were better there than dying in the kitchen where I left them.'

Jordan dropped her handbag to the floor and looked at him. 'Oh, Rhys,' she said unsteadily. And then: 'I am sorry,' and his hand shook a little as he lifted the glass to his lips.

'Are you?' he said at last, putting the empty glass back on the tray and looking at her reflection in the smoked glass above the cabinet. 'Well——' he turned abruptly to face her, 'I'll go and take that shower. Help yourself to anything you want while I'm away.'

'Can't I come with you?' With unsteady fingers, Jordan unbuttoned her coat and slipped it off her shoulders. 'I—I could wash your back. You used to like me to do that, do you remember?'

'*Jordan!*'

His agonised use of her name had a desperate ring, and although he had turned his back on her again, Jordan quickly crossed the space between them. 'I love you,' she breathed, sliding her arms around his waist and pressing her face to the male-scented suede of his jacket. 'I always have, and I always will. I was just too proud and too stubborn to admit it before.'

Rhys took a tortured breath. 'Are you sure about this?' he muttered, making no attempt to touch her, though she could tell from the rigidity of his body that it was taking all his self-control not to do so. 'Are you sure you're not just—feeling sorry for me at the moment? Lucy's going to get better. I can cope with it.'

'Oh, Rhys!' With a little groan, she buried her face against his jacket. 'Do you want me or don't you? If you've got any doubts, then tell me, because I don't think I can take much more.'

'You can't take much more!' he echoed hoarsely, pulling her round until she was facing him. 'How do you think I feel?' And holding her face between his hands, he covered her mouth with his.

There was a hungry urgency in his kiss that betrayed the depth of his feelings for her. Jordan's lips parted at the first touch of his mouth and its sensual invasion sent the blood like liquid-fire through her veins. She clung to him fervently as the white heat of his passion engulfed them both, and the moist intimacy of his mouth-to-mouth possession dispelled any lingering doubts she might have had.

'Have I answered your question?' he demanded a few minutes later, and she pressed her lips to the opened vee of his shirt, tasting his heated skin.

'Are you going to let me stay?' she breathed, parting all the buttons of his shirt, and she felt the shudder that passed through him.

'Just try to get away,' he muttered, swinging her up into his arms, and her fingers found his lips as he carried her out of the stark living room and into his bedroom.

Hours later, when they had made love and showered together, and then made love again, Jordan stirred sleepily in Rhys's arms. It was dark beyond the heavy curtains at the windows, but in the lamplit bedroom it was warm and comfortable, the downy quilt that covered them generating little more heat than the entwined closeness of their bodies.

Rhys was still sleeping, Jordan saw contentedly, turning her head on the pillow where Rhys had cushioned his face on her hair. Already he looked more relaxed—younger, she realised, with some gratification—and disarmingly vulnerable in this sensual, abandoned state.

As if he had just become aware of her innocent appraisal, Rhys's eyes opened suddenly, and his lean features took on an expression of unconcealed satisfaction. 'I was half afraid I was dreaming,' he muttered, cupping her face with his hand and bringing her mouth to his. 'Oh, love—how have I lived so long without you?'

Jordan looped her arms around his neck, loving the feel of his hair-roughened skin against hers. 'It was my fault,' she breathed. 'Blame me, not yourself. If I hadn't been so stupid, you might not have gone away.'

Rhys buried his face in her nape. 'I should have told you I'd been married. I should have told you about Jennifer.'

'Perhaps.' Jordan threaded her fingers through his hair. 'But I should have been prepared to believe you. If I'd had more faith in your feelings for me, things might have been so different.'

'It's over now.' Rhys drew back to deposit light kisses at the corners of her mouth. 'We can't undo the past. But we have got the future, if that's what you want.'

'If it's what *I* want?' Jordan gazed at him tremulously. 'Is it what *you* want?'

Rhys groaned. 'It's what I've always wanted, don't you know that?' He paused. 'Didn't Chas tell you?'

'Chas told me a lot of things.' Jordan's tongue touched his lips. 'He's very fond of you, you know.'

'Yes—well, Chas and I go back a long way,' conceded Rhys huskily. 'I guess that's why I——' He broke off and then continued unsteadily: 'Why did you come to New York, Jordan? I promise, you can tell me the truth. If it was Chas who told you, I don't care any more. Just so long as we're together, that's all I really want.'

Jordan blinked. 'No one told me about Lucy's accident, if that's what you mean. Rhys, I came—because I had to see you. I had to find out, once and for all, whether Rosa was telling the truth.'

'Rosa?' Rhys looked puzzled. 'What did Rosa tell you?'

Jordan sighed. 'She told me she thought you were still in love with me. She said she didn't think you'd been happy while you were staying on the island.' She flushed. 'She said you—drank a lot.'

Rhys's lips twisted. 'I see.'

'Wasn't it true?' Jordan looked anxious.

'About my not being happy? Oh, that was true enough,' murmured Rhys fervently, his hand sliding possessively over her breast. 'Knowing you were there, just a few miles away; hating me, as I thought—no, I wasn't happy.'

Jordan touched his cheek. 'And the drinking?'

'Some,' he conceded honestly. 'But I'm grateful to Rosa for overstating my case.'

Jordan's lips twitched. 'Oh, darling, I do love you!'

'And I love you,' he assured her roughly, his possessive exploration finding the slim curve of her hip. 'But you still didn't tell me about Chas.'

Jordan frowned. 'What about Chas?'

Rhys rolled over imprisoning her beneath him. 'When did you speak to him?' he asked softly.

Jordan's frown deepened. 'You know when. Tonight—*last* night,' she amended, realising belatedly what time it was. 'While you were visiting Lucy.' She paused, then added honestly, 'He told me about the blood test you took to prove Lucy's parentage. I hope you don't mind!'

'Oh, Jordan!' Rhys pressed his face between her breasts and she felt him shake his head. 'So you really didn't know whether Lucy was my daughter or not when you left Eleutha?'

'No.' Jordan sounded puzzled. 'Does it matter?'

'Only to me,' Rhys assured her unevenly. 'You really would have come back to me, even knowing that I might have been lying?'

Jordan cradled his face between her two hands. 'I discovered I didn't care any more,' she admitted emotionally. 'And when Chas told me about—well, I felt terrible.'

'I was a fool,' said Rhys harshly. 'As soon as I had proof, I should have come back and told you. But pride can be a damned uncomfortable thing.'

'For me, too,' murmured Jordan, nodding. 'If only Rosa hadn't said Lucy looked like you!'

Rhys's foot stroked her leg. 'Rosa has a lot to answer for,' he agreed, without rancour. 'And Lucy does have eyes like mine.' He paused. 'But so did Jack Costa.'

'Jack Costa? He's Lucy's real father?'

'Was,' said Rhys flatly. 'He was a seaman. He was drowned in a fishing accident some years ago.'

'And Lucy never knew him?'

'I doubt if she remembers him.' Rhys shook his head. 'We don't talk about it. So far as Lucy is concerned, I'm her father. I didn't want her to experience the same lack of identity I'd once suffered. That's why I took responsibility for her. It didn't seem fair that a kid of six should be made to pay for her parents' mistakes. I adopted her, you know. Just to make everything legal. Of course, she doesn't know that.'

'Oh, Rhys!' Jordan pulled him down to her. 'Do you think she'll ever accept me?'

'As her stepmother, you mean?' asked Rhys huskily.
'I think so. She asked me if I was in love with you,
you know. She's not entirely without perception.'

Jordan caught her breath. 'So Rosa wasn't lying
about that.'

'*She* told you?'

'Yes.' Jordan coloured. 'She said you didn't deny it.'

'How could I?' Rhys breathed against her cheek.
'I've always been in love with you, and now I'll never
let you go.'

The shrill peal of the telephone beside the bed
interrupted the intimate possession of his mouth, and
dragging himself away from her, Rhys stretched out a
hand to answer it.

'It's the hospital,' he mouthed, as Jordan propped
herself up on her elbows, wide-eyed and anxious.
Then: 'She has? Oh, that's great! We'll come over
right away.'

She waited, and after he had replaced the receiver,
she looked expectantly at him. 'Lucy's recovered
consciousness,' he said, pausing a moment to bestow a
lingering kiss on her parted lips. 'Come on, get your
clothes on. We're going to see her.'

'Me, too?' Jordan gazed at him.

'From now on, we're going everywhere together,'
declared Rhys huskily. 'Now, cover yourself, woman,
before I start something we don't have time to finish!'

Four months later, Jordan drove out to Heathrow
Airport to meet her stepdaughter on her return from
Eleutha. Lucy had been spending a prolonged holiday
with Karen at the hotel she was now running—with
Neil's assistance—and Jordan was looking forward to
seeing her stepdaughter again, and hearing how her
sister was managing to cope with her new re-
sponsibilities.

MOONDRIFT 185

Jordan herself looked much different from the hollow-eyed girl who had gone looking for Rhys in New York four months ago. Being married to Rhys for almost the whole of that time had returned the bloom of youth to her warm features, and their month-long honeymoon in the Seychelles had left her with the confident air of a woman who knows she is loved.

'Jordan!' Lucy came rushing out of the Customs hall into her arms, and the two girls hugged one another warmly. 'I've missed you,' Lucy declared, drawing back to look at her. 'But I'm not going to believe that you've missed me. You look fantastic! Is that mink?'

'It's sable, actually,' admitted Jordan ruefully, as the porter wheeling Lucy's luggage caught up with them. 'Do you think it's too extravagant? I told your father I didn't need another fur coat, but he insisted. What do you think?'

'I think you look beautiful,' said Lucy sincerely, looking down at her own fur-trimmed sheepskin without envy. 'It wouldn't look half as good on me. You're so tall and slim and elegant.' She paused. 'But gaining weight, if I'm not mistaken.'

Jordan felt the warm colour flood her cheeks as she directed the porter to follow them to the exit. 'I'm pregnant,' she murmured in a low tone, watching Lucy's expression anxiously. 'I wanted to tell you, before anyone else.'

'Except Daddy,' amended Lucy drily, and Jordan smiled.

'Except him,' she conceded. 'Well? Do you mind?'

Lucy preceded her through the automatic doors and grimaced humorously when she saw her stepmother's Mercedes parked on the double yellow lines. 'Why should I mind?' she asked, settling herself into the front seat and waiting for Jordan to slide in beside her.

'It's time you two had a family,' she added, as her stepmother paid the porter for stowing their luggage. 'You're not as young as you used to be, you know.'

Jordan gave a gurgling laugh and started the engine. 'Well, that's certainly true as far as I'm concerned,' she agreed, pulling the car out into the stream of traffic leaving London's busiest airport. 'And I think your father's rather pleased. He'd like more children.'

'You mean he'd like a child of his own,' remarked Lucy carelessly, as they turned west towards Oxford. 'By the way, Karen's coping really well with the hotel. And did she tell you—she and Neil have become quite close?'

Jordan blinked. She couldn't take her eyes from the road for more than a second, but Lucy's comments could not be ignored, and stepping on the brake, she pulled into the slow-moving lane of the motorway. 'What did you say?'

'Karen's managing to run——'

'Not about Karen,' said Jordan sharply. 'About your father liking a child of his own. He has you. This child I'm carrying will be your half-brother or sister.'

Lucy bent her head. 'It won't,' she said succinctly. 'I know I'm not really Da—Rhys's daughter. I've known about it for ages. Don't look so shocked. I didn't mean to upset you.'

Jordan took the next exit from the motorway, and as soon as she could, she pulled the car off the road. Then she turned to look at her stepdaughter, and Lucy leant forward to press an impulsive kiss against her cheek.

'Don't look like that,' she said. 'Daddy—Rhys—doesn't know. Oh, I wanted to tell him, but I didn't know how. I mean, how do you tell someone that you're not really their daughter? Particularly when that person has expended so much time and money and *love* upon you!'

'Oh, Lucy!' Jordan gazed at her helplessly. 'I don't know what to say.'

'Don't say anything.' Lucy bent her head. 'Just tell me you don't think Daddy will hate me for it. Could you tell him? I mean, you'd do it so much better than I could, and perhaps now he won't be too— disappointed.'

Jordan shook her head. 'Darling, your father won't be too disappointed at all.'

'Don't you think so?' Lucy looked more hopeful.

'No.' Jordan sought about for the right words. 'And he is your father, you know. He adopted you—quite legally.'

Lucy was nodding with evident relief, when the import of what her stepmother had said seemed to strike her. 'He—*adopted* me? But why did he do that?'

Jordan took Lucy's hands between her own. 'Can't you guess?'

Lucy stared at her, comprehension dawning in her eyes. 'He knows?'

'He knows,' agreed Jordan softly. 'But what he'll want to know is, how do you?'

Lucy swallowed convulsively. 'He really knows? He's known all these years?'

'Yes.' Jordan hesitated. 'He and your mother were separated at the time you were conceived. He knew you couldn't be his daughter.'

Lucy shook her head. 'But why did he——'

'He loved you,' said Jordan simply. 'He cared about you, and he didn't want you to be hurt by what had happened to your mother.'

'Oh, isn't he wonderful!' breathed Lucy, her eyes shining with unshed tears. Then she sniffed. 'But will he forgive me for not being honest with him?'

Jordan sighed. 'I think so. But you still haven't told me how you found out.' She paused. 'You weren't old enough to understand.'

Lucy lifted her shoulders. 'Not then, no. But later I was.'

Jordan frowned. 'Someone told you?'

'No.' Lucy shook her head. Then she went on: 'When Daddy came to see me in the hospital—after the plane crash, you know?—he brought Mummy's suitcase with him. It had survived the crash, I don't know how. Like me, I suppose. Anyway, there were things in it, things that had been Mummy's, which he thought I might like to keep. Among them was a photograph of me, when I was a baby. In a frame.'

'Go on.'

'Well——' Lucy wetted her lips, 'I didn't touch the photograph at first. When Daddy took me to live with him, it was all so strange at first, and I was still upset about Mummy. Oh, he—Daddy, that is—he helped me a lot. But she was my mother, after all, and I was only six.' She shook her head reminiscently. 'It wasn't until I was about nine or ten that I discovered what was in the back of the photograph.'

'What was it?' asked Jordan doubtfully. 'A letter?'

'No. My birth certificate,' admitted Lucy unhappily. 'Mummy must have put it there and forgotten about it. Anyway, my father's name was given as Jack Costa—Uncle Jack, that is. We used to live with him before we started looking for—for Rhys. Maybe my mother thought that by putting Uncle Jack's name on the certificate she'd have some hold on him afterwards, but it didn't work that way. I still remember the rows there were before he left. Then one day he didn't come back.'

'Oh, Lucy!'

I tore it up,' said Lucy, with a sudden shiver. 'The

birth certificate, I mean. I didn't want Daddy—
Rhys—to send me back to Uncle Jack, so I burnt the
pieces. It was silly, I realise that now, but I thought if
I destroyed the evidence . . .' She broke off. 'I was
only nine years old. I never dreamed Daddy might
know the truth.'

'Oh, sweetheart, you had no need to worry.' With a
shake of her head, Jordan gathered the girl into her
arms and hugged her. 'Come on, let's go home. Your
father will be wondering where we are—not to
mention Mrs Settle! I may be the new mistress of your
father's house, but you're still the apple of her eye.'

'. . . and that's what she's been hiding all these years,'
finished Jordan huskily, snuggling down on Rhys's
knee. 'Poor Lucy. She didn't have to tell me, but—she
felt she had to.'

'She wanted to,' essayed Rhys, depositing a warm
kiss at the corner of her mouth. 'I guess she cares
more about you than you realised.'

'And you're not angry, are you?' Jordan ventured
softly. 'I mean, I promised her you wouldn't be.'

'Did you?' Rhys looked down at his wife's reclining
form with disturbing eyes. 'Is that why you chose to
wear this revealing negligee? To prove that if I was
angry, you were prepared to suffer the inevitable
consequences?'

'Promises, promises,' breathed Jordan, the sleeves
of her gown falling back as she wound her arms
around his neck. 'No, seriously, darling——'

'Seriously, I want to make love to you,' he told her
firmly, and Jordan submitted to the searching pressure
of his lips without objection.

'But do you mind about Lucy?' she whispered a few
moments later, and he groaned and rested his face in
the hollow of her neck.

'I hope she appreciates what a staunch ally she has in you,' he muttered. 'I'll talk to Lucy tomorrow. And I promise to be gentle. Does that satisfy you?' He paused. 'Now, do you want to help me to undress, hmm?'

Jordan's cheeks dimpled. 'At your service, oh Lord and Master!' Diligently she unfastened all the buttons on his shirt, and slid her hands inside next to his warm skin. 'Hmm, you always smell so nice . . .'

'So do you,' retorted Rhys, his hands invading the neckline of the revealing negligee. 'You know, I've missed you today. The sooner that sound studio on Eleutha is completed, the better I shall like it.'

Jordan pressed her lips to his throat. 'You're lazy,' she breathed, and Rhys chuckled.

'Only jealous of every minute you're out of my sight,' he told her thickly. 'I don't think the Settles will see much of us once I can work on the island.'

'But we'll still keep this place, won't we?' she asked, looking round the lemon and gold luxury of their bedroom. Rhys's house, set in the Oxfordshire countryside, had been their first real home together, and she didn't want to lose it. 'We've been so happy here.'

'If that's what you want,' Rhys conceded, propelling her to her feet. 'And Lucy's getting older. She may prefer to work in England.'

'Somehow I think Lucy sees certain advantages to living on Eleutha,' said Jordan happily, sliding Rhys's shirt off his shoulders. 'Steve's going to help his father in running the importing company next year when he leaves school. Lucy told me as we drove back from the airport.'

'Seems like Lucy told you a lot of things,' remarked Rhys drily, stepping out of his trousers.

'Well, I am her stepmother,' Jordan reminded him huskily, and Rhys pulled her urgently to him.

'And my child's mother,' he added, his hands seeking and finding the distinct swell of her abdomen.

'You do understand about Lucy, don't you?' she asked anxiously. 'After the way she took our relationship, I wouldn't want to hurt her.'

'My love, Lucy could see no fun in living with me without you. From the minute I saw you again, I became quite intolerable.'

'Even so——'

'Even so, I won't hurt her feelings, I promise. Poor kid, she must have been scared stiff.'

'When she found out? Yes, I think she was. She was so afraid you might send her back to Jack Costa.'

'I'd never have done that.'

'Then tell her,' said Jordan huskily. 'That's all she wants to hear.'

'Hmm.' Rhys touched her mouth with his fingers. 'She has a lot to thank you for.'

'And you,' said Jordan breathily, as he tugged the cord of her robe free and gazed with evident approval at the honeyed beauty of her rounded body.

'We've got so much,' he muttered unsteadily, pulling her towards him. 'And this time I don't intend to let it go ...'

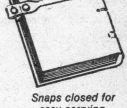